I0618697

Make No Assumptions

GLENDA MACE KOTCHISH

JANE ELLEN HOLLIDAY WILSON

ISBN: 0998971502
ISBN-13: 978-0998971506

DEDICATION

To our friend and mentor, Joan Garrabrant.

CONTENTS

FORWARD

MAKE NO ASSUMPTIONS

Make no assumptions that your perspective will be mine.
We may both be Southerners, both have grown up within
miles of one another, gone to rival high schools within
shouting distance, both had difficult first marriages, raised
two children, found love at last....
.....But that doesn't mean that we write the same stories,
about the same things.

Make No Assumptions is an anthology comprised of stories
we wrote together. Over a year, we met every Wednesday
and chose a topic. Both of us wrote whatever struck our
fancy—poetry, short stories, memoir, or a combination of
them all. Then we went home and feverishly developed,
edited and developed some more, as all writers must.
So sit back in an easy chair with a nice glass of iced tea
(sweet of course), and enjoy.

Janie and Glenda

THE ENCOUNTER
Glenda Mace Kotchish

She spoke quietly and slowly, looking directly at him.

"It's not you.

"It's not yours. It doesn't pertain to you--at all."

"Whatever it is that I'm feeling is *me*, mine, belonging exclusively to me."

She took a breath and continued, "This is how the world communicates. The words may be directed toward you and seem to be *for* you--about you--and even the pronoun "you" and sometimes *your name* will be called out amidst it all. *But*, understand, it is *not* about you."

This is how she began the conversation with him.

He opened his mouth to speak but she moved close to him and raised her index finger. She placed it to his lips-- almost touching. "Shh--don't speak," she whispered.

He was startled. He did not know her, and so he took one step back in the tiny elevator.

She held his eyes with hers, and placed that same index finger on her lips.

"Shh, not a word, please."

The elevator doors opened and she turned around and stepped out. She walked away without even a glance back.

CHAPTER 1 FENCES

GLENDA KOTCHISH and JANE WILSON

It Was a Fence

Jane Ellen Holliday Wilson

It was just a fence—a wonderful three-board fence, perfect for climbing up and sitting on, on a sunny day. Or was it more...

What was I straddling that day--two worlds, or maybe more; black/white, servant/master, girl rules/boy rules? I was oblivious to all of this as I sat there in the glorious sunshine a few months beyond my fifth birthday—probably mid-July or such—clad in my favorite overalls, waist-length blond curls blessedly wound up in a bun, barefoot and loving life. (Momma was already worried, "This *farm life* is making a wild animal of that girl." I had no idea what she meant when I overheard her telling Daddy this.)

For once no one was looking for me. No chores were waiting for me. No sisters were casting me as *the baby* in their latest play. The cat was probably filling in for me, poor thing.

I was free to sit there, and I was fascinated. The *men* (as we always called them)—farm hands sent over by the owner of our rented farm—were in the hay field. They had a marvelous contraption attached to the old John Deere.

I heard it before I saw it. It was in the field early. And when I came down to breakfast, Daddy answered my curiosity, "It's called a hay baler and it's magic, little girl. You'll have to go out and see how it works after breakfast." Then he was off to inspect dairies all over the county. (Daddy made sure our milk was clean, and we girls were very proud of him for that.)

As I sat there on the fence watching, the machine

rolled over the field and out popped perfect rectangles of hay. It kept happening over and over again. I was captivated. These men, this marvelous machine, and this beautiful day were indeed *magical* to me, just as Daddy had promised.

One of the *men* was a clown-like character. Now that I'm older, it is easy enough to see that he loved an audience. On that day it just seemed like Mr. Green Jeans from the Captain Kangaroo Show had showed up in my own back yard, just for me. (My short life, lived mostly on this two hundred acre patch of land, did not afford much exposure to people of any kind, other than my two sisters and my parents.)

So there he was, Mr. Green Jeans, dancing across the field, grabbing the heavy bales and loading them on the flatbed truck that followed along behind the baler. He waved to me over and over again as they went by. And I waved back every time. He and his fellow workers seemed so happy. It was like we were caught in a mysterious bubble of happiness.

I remember it as one of the sunniest, sweetest, most wholesome mornings of my life until…

Until Momma—a city girl by all accounts—came running out to get me, "Katie Scott, you stop talking to those men right now, and get down from there this minute. Go on and get back in the house."

Slam—my reverie was busted. "Momma, why? Why do I have to get down? I'm having so much fun. Look at that machine! It's magic," I said, pointing at the marvelous baler still chugging away in the field.

"This is not the time to talk back to me young lady, you just go on and get back in the house."

As I look back now at that moment in what would have been 1962, I think it was the beginning of my *fence straddling* (common in our little rural Virginia town). I would find myself wobbling on this sort of precipice often. The world was changing. We children already knew it, long before the adults around us could comprehend it.

Still it would be many years before I would come to understand the tension between my child-like wide-open wonder, and my mother's deep-seated fears for the little girls she loved so fiercely. Many fences separated us, many were straddled and occasionally, just occasionally, she came to sit with me and enjoy the sunshine on a precarious fence or two.

The Last Fence

Glenda Mace Kotchish

It is the last fence standing...anywhere--in the whole country, north, south, east and west. It is an anomaly, left over from the time when there were border fences to keep out the would-be immigrants, fences to keep cattle and sheep within the bounds of the commercial ranches, fences to keep the prisoners within the walls of the penal communities, fences that divided the residential gardens, backyards, fishing reserves, zoos. All have been gone for fifty years now--the need for fences is past, except, that is, for this one, the last fence.

Molly is astonished when she discovers it, or rather when Lexi discovers it while chasing the hare now entangled in the loose wires.

"Stop Lexi," she shouts as she sprints to the bramble of vines and undergrowth where the dog is alternately barking and snapping. Although Molly is sixty years old, her elected-age is thirty-four, and she arrives in seconds before harm is done to the wild creature--so rare to find animals in the countryside in 2115.

You heard right--*elected age*. Ain't it just great? Pick the age that you like best. If you have enough connections and can provide the documentation to substantiate your outstanding potential and contributions to the betterment of society, you get to stay as young (or old) as you see fit. Women typically pick their thirties. But men select their twenties--not for the reason you might guess, (well that too) but because mathematical and scientific breakthroughs are more likely to come to the twenty-something male mind.

"What have we here? Poor little critter," Molly says as she stoops to size up the situation. Lexi barks and races uncontrollably behind her.

She lifts the chain link wire trapping the hare and it scampers madly away. Molly grabs hold of Lexi's collar who, otherwise, would be in hot pursuit. "Sorry girl but fun's over. That poor little guy is scared to death. Stay, now." Lexi sits obediently as Molly rises.

"A fence. Who would have guessed? Most people don't know what this is. It's in pretty good shape except for this bottom here," Molly says out loud as she steps back to examine the relic.

The fence is wrought iron of intricate design. Chain link is attached to the bottom of the fence and looks as though it goes into the ground below the fence.

Molly raises her index finger to the outer corner of her right eye and gently presses. She moves her gaze over the fence and again presses the corner of her eye. She then touches and taps her left ring finger. "Call Bryan," she says and waits.

In a few seconds a voice says "Hey, Molly. What on earth have you sent me?"

"Bryan, believe it or not I think I might have found a fence and a beautiful one at that."

"Do another scan Molly, this time--live so I can get a good look," Bryan excitedly answers.

Molly touches the corner of her eye and blinks twice. "How's this? Here's where it's grounded," she says as she points to the chain link section. She moves her gaze slowly upward.

"Stop there," says Bryan.

"This relic may be charcoal iron, at first glance. Which means it must have been imported from Europe before the industrial age puddle-iron method. I can't confirm that without some tests." Bryan says.

"Do you happen to have your PCS on you?" he asks.

"No, sorry. But there's just not enough sunlight to get a reading of the photochemical smog. You have my location. Why not join me and we can test it together?

"Some museum is going to be happy with this discovery. What an antiquity!" Molly says.

"Some museum, or the Metals and Gems Agency. Are you on public or private land?" Bryan asks.

"Maybe public, but Lexi found it and strayed off the path a bit, so I'm not sure. I'll run a quick check of this location. I'll wait here for you," Molly says.

"I can't believe we found this. Anyone else may not have known what it is, and what a treasure of past times." Molly marvels.

"I know. I'll be there soon--about an hour. Settle back and wait for me. I'll bring the kits. You can research the location and restrictions codes, and use of the area while you wait," Bryan says and then disconnects.

Molly sits down and touches the corner of her eye, adjusts her contacts for connect-mode and begins the research. Documents and images appear in her lens. She blinks to move forward and back through the sites.

"The question is, Lexi, do we save the fence for display in a museum, leave it here as a relic or make use of the material so desperately needed?" Lexi sits beside her and dozes off.

Sitting quietly, Molly scans the connection and within ten minutes locates the property and court records for ownership. She discovers the fence is in fact on private property.

Lexi who has been sleeping, raises her head and her ears point up. She stands, and the hair on her back rises. She makes a low growl in her throat.

"What do you hear, girl?" Molly says as she takes hold of Lexi's collar. Molly looks up to see three figures standing over her. The next thing she knows she is on the other side of the fence which is now glowing blue. Lexi is nowhere in sight. She turns around in a circle. The fence is also circling her. She walks to it but when she approaches pulses flare.

"What's happening?" Molly says. "This is not good. Lexi, Lexi," she calls out but there is only silence except for the hum of light-particles.

She taps her left finger, "Call Bryan." She waits-- nothing. She tries again. She keeps trying over and over tapping her finger, calling Bryan frantically, until her finger is red and bruised. At last she hears a buzz.

"Molly, finally! I've been waiting here for you. Where are you?" the voice of Bryan comes through.

"Oh thank goodness," Molly says. "I'm on the other side of the fence. I don't know how I got here but Lexi's not here and the fence has a current running through it."

"What fence?" Bryan says. I'm standing at the exact GPS location you sent me but there's nothing here except a few rabbit holes--which is odd in itself, but nothing else. Lexi is here with me, and I can't calm her down. Shoot me your location."

Molly touches the left corner of her eye and scans the horizon. "Did you get it?"

"No nothing, yet. Try again," Bryan answers.

"Ok. Here goes," Molly says as she scans the horizon and transmits. "How's that?"

"No, nothing," Bryan answers. And then his voice is gone, only the sound of static remains."

The fence glows white and radiates, the whiteness turns to fog and sizzles and slowly edges inward toward Molly.

Molly's adrenaline rises and she swallows, the taste of metal in her mouth makes her stomach flip.

"Bryan, this is scary," she says, knowing he can't hear her.

"Hello, hello," she calls out to no one. "Hey, let's just cut the crap. Sure I got on your land--sorry but it was an accident."

The low humming sounds continue.

"Hey I'm sorry. Really. Can you cut the light show?

Please," she pleads.

She sits down on the ground. The fog is above her. She takes deep breaths and tries to calm herself.

And as quickly as it began, the fog is gone, the fence is gone, the blue and white lights are gone. There stands Bryan--20 feet away. Lexi races across the field, ignoring the hares, she jumps onto Molly. Molly burrows her face into Lexi's neck.

"Molly, quick--stand up, come here. Now!" Bryan shouts.

Molly and Lexi run to Bryan.

"It was horrific. I was trapped. I couldn't see you and the fence, the fence is--well where is the damn fence?" Molly looks around confused.

"I don't know, Molly. But there is something very odd about this spot.

The ground rumbles.

"Let's get back on the path." Brian picks up a handful of soil and puts it in his pocket.

Molly looks at him. "For the lab," he says as he grabs her hand. They hurry back to the path as the ground behind them falls away.

CHAPTER 2 FASCINATING PLACES

GLENDA KOTCHISH and JANE WILSON

The Remarkable Island

Glenda Mace Kotchish

It is hot and humid on the island, today. There is no breeze. Tess looks out the window of her little cottage. Drops of sweat run down her back. Normally she would complain to herself about the weather, but today she is oddly tolerant of its effects.

The island. It has its extremes in shockingly short segments and lightning fast changeovers. This is one of the humid seasons. The air is heavy with moisture--close to rain without actually raining, and just as heavy with insects of all varieties: crawling, flying, creeping, rolling and the inert ones pretending to be twigs, stones, orchids and even cabbages. They know their season is short and take full advantage of the prime conditions to hatch out, eat, sting, bite, suck, lay eggs; and then it's over for them--leaving the place to their offspring--when the next favorable season rolls around.

"So much time spent trying to predict what the change will be and when," Tess thinks as she checks the thermostat--98 degrees. She slips on a cotton shift and sandals. She gathers her bag and purse--locks the door behind her as she leaves.

She does not look back--just opens the gate and walks straight to the dock. She hears the gate latch behind her, as it swings shut. The ferry is waiting.

"Right on time," Fred calls out, "not a minute too soon or too late," he says as he takes her bag and helps her aboard.

"Thanks Fred," she says. "It looks like the right day to

make the crossing, but you never know."

"That's a fact--you never know--strangest thing I've ever seen, this island. You should be glad to leave I'd think," he says as he backs the boat out of the dock.

"You're not the only one on board," he calls out and nods his head to the stern. "Two families are quitting it today."

He works the throttle and watches the channel.

"It's been awhile since I seen a whole family leave. And two at once, well that there's what I'd call *remarkable*. Usually it's the wife and kids what leaves. The husband stays, at least for a while anyways."

Tess nods. "Sometimes you *know* when you're done, I guess. And sometimes, well you hope things will turn around as you planned."

"So it is, so it is," Fred says. "And I'm guessing you're saying *you're* done."

"Yep," Tess says. She turns to leave. "I'm going to find myself a seat and put this behind me--as it were. Nice talking with you, Fred."

"You bet ya," he replies.

Tess makes her way to the rows of seats on deck. There are a couple of spaces left. She settles herself beside a little boy about seven years old. She smiles and says, "Hi."

"Hi," he says and he turns to look back at the island that is disappearing from view.

Tess stows her bag and purse under the seat and leans her head back on the padded headrest. The island--a tiny dot on the horizon--is suddenly gone. The mainland is, of course, nowhere in sight. The wind begins to blow a welcomed, cooling breeze although the sky remains hazy. Tess glances at the little boy beside her. He is still staring at the place where the island was. She takes a breath and slowly lets it out--then closes her eyes.

She thinks back to the time spent in the little house on the island when she first arrived--what seems like a lifetime ago. How many years *has* it been? It's hard to say--with the seasons changing as they do--in no particular pattern. Her queries about the phenomenon had been either met with, "That's the way of things here," or with complicated and convoluted scientific speculation ranging from the location of the island in the earth's electromagnetic field, to volcanic material and gasses shifting and releasing into the atmosphere, to the most fantastic, time warp--from Star Trek, Star Wars types, and transcendentalists. Tess argues with the latter that the island cannot be in a time warp since anyone can board the ferry and leave anytime one wishes.

"Baffling," she says.

"What?" a small voice asks.

Tess opens her eyes. "Oh, I'm sorry. I was thinking out loud," she says to the little boy next to her.

"What's baffling?" he asks.

"The island--weather and seasons," she answers.

"Oh that," he says. "I like it."

Tess tilts her head in thought. After a moment she says, "Me too."

"But my Mom," the boy continues, "She says she doesn't like it because she can't plan anything."

"Oh? Like what?" Tess asks.

"Like picnics or birthday parties or even Christmas--especially Christmas. She likes to have snow, and the tree, and to make me wool hats. But you never know what it will be like on the day--so she gets mad and makes a fuss."

"Where's your Mom?" Tess asks leaning her head forward and looking at the seats to the right of the boy.

"She's still on the island," he answers.

"I'm going to get a soda," he says as he hops up out of his seat.

Tess watches him walk to the cabin, open the door and disappear inside. She sighs. "I'm feeling very tired--but not weary," she thinks, "as though I just got over the flu and it's my first day of feeling good--good but weak." She leans her head back and closes her eyes again.

The boat rocks and the steady noise of the engine lull her to sleep. She dreams she sees the families and passengers walk about the deck and go into the cabin. She sleeps deeply and long until a cool wind wakens her. She smiles as she feels the moisture evaporate from her skin with its cooling effect. She opens her eyes--glad for the change. After a few moments she stands, stretches her arms out and then over her head and yawns a big yawn. She glances around. There is no one on deck--just herself.

"I feel so good," she says. "Yes, it's a good day to leave--a very good day."

She walks to the cabin door, turns the knob and steps into the darkness.

SOLITUDE

Jane Ellen Holliday Wilson

Its name was so apt for what it was to me--Solitude.

The moment I walked through the doors I felt I had arrived home in some strange, unspoken way--home to the person I really was--the person I could be. No, the person I *would* be for the rest of my life.

It was a charming old place. White clapboard, low and long, perfectly proportioned, complete with tin roof, creaky pine floors, windows to the floor and fireplaces-- ancient shabby elegance resting beside its own little pond on the edge of campus.

At the time, I knew nothing of its history--or my own really. Would I have understood its draw more clearly had I realized then that my ancestors may well have lived in this cozy house centuries before? Were they drawing me here now? Had they been luring me back to these mountains all my life? Or was it something else? All I knew then was that Solitude was where I wanted to be.

I *did* know that it wasn't just Solitude's cozy farmhouse beauty that drew me. It was, even more so, what was found inside. Strewn all around, in a manner that only a designer could appreciate were sumptuous fabric samples, velvety carpet scraps, bulky wallcovering books, some rather strange and inventive furniture, and bizarre lighting fixtures--the kind of cast-offs that product reps left behind for aspiring design students to ponder and play with.

These sumptuous materials were just waiting to be applied to mat boards using the dangerously dull mat knives and noxious smelling, half empty gluing spray cans sitting around on drafting tables everywhere. Partially raided Rapidograph pen sets would be carefully unclogged to use to letter on descriptions, while drafting pencils would create floor plans, elevations, and perspective drawings. These were the tools of my soon-to-be trade, and I could hardly wait to get my hands on them.

Finally, I had made it to this place. Two years of prerequisites--math, chemistry, architectural history, anatomy, business, art--had won me my spot among a select group of a dozen or so design students. We were a determined bunch. All of us had to work hard to get here. It was good to be together. Labeled *special thinkers*, by our kindest teachers--the kids with visual, multidimensional brains--none of us were conventional learners. But it turned out that we were exactly who we needed to be in order to master design school. You know the type--very strong on the right side of the brain. We knew we were different, and we also knew that we were passionate about design. And now, *finally*, we were free to pursue that common passion; speak our common language.

Together, for the next two years we had a place of our own--our own, alluring

...Solitude.

CHAPTER 3 IT'S RELATIVE

GLENDA KOTCHISH and JANE WILSON

Great Grandmama's Front Porch

Jane Ellen Holliday Wilson

Great Grandmama Lucie had a big front porch--big enough to hold everybody--or so it seemed to me as a little girl in the early 60's. It was sturdy, solid, deep and wide in the way of so many Roanoke, Virginia homes, with a sloping red tin roof and cement floor painted the color of the winter sky, and rimmed with substantial brick half walls capped with pristine white wood ledges. This was where the gentlemen propped themselves to discuss their politics and their work at the railroad. The ladies took the proper seats--white wicker chairs and settees. Grandmama Lucie held court in her big rocker.

We children would jostle for spots on the two porch swings, hoping that soon Great Aunt Clara would show up with lemonade and those confectioners sugar covered wedding cookies. In no time at all that sugar would cover our neatly starched, home from church pinafores, dresses and even our ruffled white socks.

Wedding cookies! Already they thrilled us girls, filling our heads with visions of white lace dresses and flower bouquets, bridesmaids and handsome boys dressed up in tuxedos.

As the men gathered among the begonias on the porch ledge, filling, then lighting their pungent pipes--tobacco grown just down the road, Aunt Clara settled in to play with us little ones. With a merry gleam in her eye, she would start the games: *Eenie-meenie-miney-mo*, *I've got a secret* and some other silly games she used to coax us into playing.

27

This was her way of getting her nieces and nephews to share little bits of us with her; and each other. We were shy of each other, brought together from all over the place--big cities, little towns, country farms--and we hadn't a clue what to say to one another until Aunt Clara wound us up and got us going, wearing down the barriers around us, and weaving us into the close-knit family she already understood us to be.

Looking back, this porch sitting may have only happened once or twice, maybe three times. But how important such innocent moments are in the life of a child. Like a veritable United Nations there on Grandmama Lucie's porch, my family was letting us know that, no matter how small or vulnerable we were, we had a place in this world, a value beyond school work and the relative shine on our excruciatingly uncomfortable Mary-Janes.

A Child's Easter

Glenda Mace Kotchish

Easter. Finally the girls were allowed to wear white shoes--until Labor Day that is. The three sisters, Brenda, Kay and Sylvia would be outfitted in new spring dresses, which meant a whole day spent shopping--walking to town, going from store to store--the shoe store, the dress store, the larger department store and even the five-and-dime for a little treat. And then they'd take the bus home carrying boxes and bags of spring delights.

Sylvia, the youngest, was allowed to choose between a navy blue sailor dress, with white trim and a red tie and, a pink and white checked dress with short sleeves, a round elasticized neck and a ruffle at the bottom. It was a hard choice but she went with the pink. White shoes and socks, tiny little gloves and a small drawstring purse that came with the dress completed the outfit. The older girls, Brenda and Kay, got their dresses from a different dress shop, as did their mother. Then they went to the department store to buy stockings, garter belts and crinolines. Oh to have a crinoline--the *ultimate* in underwear. Sylvia's slip was a "full slip", with straps and only a slight stiffness. How she wanted a crinoline--layers and layers of toile. She'd even settle for white.

"Sylvia, you have no hips and can't hold up a crinoline. You need the straps. Now, now this is a fine little slip. See the pretty lace," her mother consoled her. (By the time Sylvia got hips, crinolines would probably be out of style.)

At Butlers shoe store, they walked past the saddle oxfords and loafers and went straight to the dress shoes. Kitten pumps for the older girls, high heels for mother, and white strapped flat shoes with a little bow held together with a mother-of pearl button for Sylvia.

Hats were not on the list--just a nice barrette or bow. Mother liked to show off her beautiful shoulder length, brown hair, and her girls' blonde curls as well.

Saturday night before Easter morning, mother rolled individual sections of Sylvia's hair in brown paper strips. The next morning, the papers would be removed to form ringlets. The older girls pin curled their own hair as did Mother. When the bobby pins were removed, the curls would be softly brushed out to form waves, curled under at the ends.

Easter preparations were not complete until two-dozen eggs were dyed--orange, blue, yellow, red, pink and purple. The egg-dying kit came with decals that could be applied with a soft rag, dipped in vinegar and gently pressed over the paper onto the eggs. The eggs were placed in a bowl on a bed of green cellophane grass and put in the refrigerator ready for tomorrow's egg hunt. The Easter outfits were taken from the closet and hung on the door hooks, ready for Easter Sunday.

"Get up Sylvia. Rise and shine," Mother said on Easter morning. She raised the shades to the bedroom windows and the morning light came flooding in.

"It's going to be a beautiful Easter this year, Sylvia. Come see what's in the living room for you."

With that, Sylvia hopped from her bed. In the living room, her sisters were already rummaging through their Easter baskets. The remaining basket, wrapped in pink cellophane was the biggest basket Sylvia had ever seen, filled with green grass, chocolates, a bunny, jelly beans and peeps.

On the coffee table sat a fancy chocolate Easter egg for

Mother and an orchid corsage that she would wear on her suit. Daddy was responsible for all of these treasures. Sylvia was glad to see he had not forgotten Mother. Forgetting Mother was not something agreeable and could (and had in the past) spoil a holiday for everyone.

Last year Daddy had forgotten Mother. Sylvia had ended up hiding the Easter eggs in the backyard herself, and then pretending not to know where they were hidden, she found them all--alone. The family did not go to church that year. The only bright spot came from the neighbor lady next door. She complimented Sylvia on how pretty her hair looked.

Oh, but yes, this year it was going to be a fine Easter.

Breakfast was a hurried affair followed by the hustle and bustle of dressing for church. Daddy was the first to finish. He waited in the living room, smoking a cigarette and reading the Sunday paper. He smelled of Old Spice and tobacco. The older girls helped Sylvia dress, and finally everyone was ready. Mother was beautiful in her pale blue suit, pearls and gloves. Daddy pinned the corsage on her lapel. And everyone piled in the car for the short ride to church.

Sylvia loved Sunday school--the stories on the felt board; the red, blue and gold stars given out for remembering to bring your Sunday school book, another for having read the story. At the very end of the lesson, the coloring pages were distributed and boxes of crayons laid out. The little girls removed their gloves to color-- inside the lines. The boys--mostly scribbled.

Then the family would meet in the sanctuary. Everyone sang "Holy, Holy, Holy" while the organ played. Then announcements were made, more singing and the passing of the silver offering plates, with their felted insides (so the coins wouldn't clink as Daddy had once explained). The flowers in the church--white lilies--were beautiful. The Pastor dressed in his robe and special white scarf (Daddy says it's a stole) gave a short sermon. (Once the Pastor and his wife came to the house for Sunday dinner. The wife wore a shiny, gold colored dress with a pointy collar. Sylvia didn't like it, even though it had a huge crinoline.)

The entire service was over in an hour--precisely, including the communion (which Sylvia did not get to do until she became "saved"). Mother had gotten saved and gave up smoking. Daddy still smoked, so she guessed he hadn't gotten saved yet either, even though he did take one of the little glasses of grape juice and a cracker.

After church it was off to Mother's sister's house for dinner. Mother brought a cake and a ham, and of course, the eggs for hiding. Mother had three sisters. Daddy didn't like any of them. Helen was "mean as a snake" he once told mother. He steered clear of her. Irene was the oldest and " bossy". Doris was the youngest and "lived in a different century," Daddy said. But Sylvia liked her cousins (when they weren't teasing her) and had a grand time playing hide and seek, rover red rover and egg hunt. The older cousins and her sisters listened to the radio and read magazines, but they did hide the eggs, so that was something.

Before dark, Mother announced it was time to go home, which meant they'd get to eat some candy from their Easter baskets. Sylvia was the first in the car and waited for the good byes. No one hugged each other, just said goodbye. The men shook hands. The women waved.

At home Sylvia ate some of her chocolate bunny and some jellybeans. And finally, it was time for bed. Tomorrow she would get her sisters to hide some of the candy eggs from her basket and she'd find them.

Soon she'd get to wear shorts, (she liked the green ones best); and to ride her bike in the alley; and make some tents in the backyard with blankets; and make mud pies in the iron skillet Daddy had given her; and maybe go fishing with Daddy. As she snuggled into her pillow, she smiled-- the best Easter--ever.

Of Handkerchiefs and Lullabies

Jane Ellen Holliday Wilson

Willy had died. He was our own faithful *Nana dog* like the one from *Peter Pan*. You know, that overseeing babysitter of a faithful dog. He had followed the children everywhere they went, staying on the doorsteps of playmates until it was time to go home. He was their first word, and the last thing they saw before bedtime. Always in the room with us, his aim was to please, and please us he had done for ten long and faithful years.

We bought him with our wedding money, and named him after my husband's father (and Prince William, Diana's new baby boy). We called him our only son. He had been my daughter's first word. Our whole neighborhood loved him. We all cried at his passing, and two months later, we wept again my family wept yet again as my marriage dissolved around us.

Here I was 39 years old, two young daughters, no dog, and no husband. My girls (and I) had lost our faithful friend and their father's presence in our home all in a matter of months--hard months. Their father wasn't coming back. There was nothing to be done about that. But I could fill the hole of Willy's loss with a new puppy. It would be a great distraction, and something fun to look forward to, or so I thought.

I began to scour the papers (no internet in those days) and soon found a dog just like Willy--a lab-golden mix puppy, the last one in the litter, only an hour away. He had to be picked up on Sunday. Sunday, the day the girl's dad was coming to get the rest of his things. The new puppy "family member" was the perfect distraction for all of us. A fresh start. A new puppy for our new threesome; a new focus, some *now* to hold us in place; a new place, momentarily free of the struggles and sorrows that had led us here.

Off we went to gather our bundle of black fur and begin the process of welcoming a new brother to the family--a new man of the house--Bubba we called him. I remember how we all sat on the floor passing him back and forth laughing away the sting in our hearts.

But it wasn't long before we realized that Bubba was no Willy. If a dog can be aggressive Bubba took the cake. Clothes were nipped and ripped, cats were chased, and children scared to death. The vet took one look at him and said, "You girls are in over your heads with this guy. I think you better start exploring obedience school."

On the way home from our first class, Bubba ate the seatbelts out of the back of the car. Things were not going well. My masterfully planned *replacement* dog was not going to be the joyful new beginning I was hoping for. What were we to do with this wild beast we had on our hands?

Thankfully, we did discover one place where such a creature might be accepted, even sought after--police school. Bubba was going to serve his country. The deal was that I had to drive him (in the car with no seatbelts, mind you) two hours away into the country to drop him off never to be seen again. Two long hours to think on-- wallow in--relive all the failures of my present life. This is where my daddy comes into the tale of the over-rambunctious wagging tail.

Even though I thought I could do this on my own-- brave, half dead girl that I was--Daddy knew better. He always did.

The man who had kissed me with tears in his eyes before walking me down the aisle; who had brought coffee in the middle of some dark and lonely nights; who had done so many things to try to help save our marriage, now was engaged in a new effort--saving what was left, my girls and me. In his ever-present, quiet-yet-emphatic way,

Daddy said, "I'm just not going to let you drive up there with that dog all alone, and that's that."

So, off we went together, me a bit begrudging the company. I really don't know how I would have managed without him. The drive alone was a challenge. There were no crates in those days, and I ended up having to ride in the back seat to keep Bubba "under control."

By the time we arrived at the facility, my arms were a bit chewed up, my clothes were a wreck, and I was finally convinced that this had to be. But first Bubba had to pass the test. My vet had told us that most dogs didn't because, once domesticated they were generally too docile to be trained to search and serve with the ferocity needed to do the job.

Immediately they took Bubba away to be tested. The policeman said, "This is it. We can't afford to mess around with these dogs. If he passes the test you aren't allowed to speak to him again. It's important for the training that the break from the former owner be complete and immediate."

I hadn't expected this. I was frightened that they wouldn't take him, and just as frightened that they would. Daddy stood close by me, telling me stories, joking around to distract me. His handkerchief was already out of his pocket when the policeman returned. (How did he know?)

"We are going to keep him ma'am."

"Can't I see him just one more time?" Tears began to trickle down my face. Daddy began to wipe them, handing the handkerchief over for me to keep.

"No ma'am, it's not good for the dog. And frankly, it's not good for the owner either."

"Can you at least contact us, write us, call us to tell us how he is doing, where he goes?" I was shaking a little by then. Daddy's arm went around my shoulder, as the tears began to gush and my nose began to dribble.

"No ma'am. It's against regulations. I'm afraid the best thing for you to do right now is to get in that car with your father and head on home."

Gently, capably, Daddy loaded me into the front seat of the car and began the long drive home. How he wove tales and sang songs all the way. Lullabies they were to me; as sure as if I were still a little girl in his arms. His deep, rich church-choir-honed voice lulled me, soothed me and helped me to know that I was not alone; that all my days would not be sad days; that there was still a man in my life, one that I could count on, one that my little girls could count on, too. We were going to be OK.

So, ask me why now, so many years later, why I am willing to sacrifice hard won professional standing, a career of some renown; more successful than I ever dreamed possible, frankly; in order to cart him around to doctors' appointments, to hold his hand as the dementia sets in, driving him to the Dollar Store to get candy, telling him over and over again what he has just forgotten five times in a row, singing him silly songs with my not so rich, not church-choir-honed voice…. and this is what I will tell you, "My daddy gave me handkerchiefs when I needed them most, and sang me lullabies."

CHAPTER 4 LET'S DO LUNCH

GLENDA KOTCHISH and JANE WILSON

LET'S DO LUNCH

Glenda Mace Kotchish

Let's do lunch,
early,
because I missed breakfast.
You see,
the dog needed a walk and
I needed a shower,
and because someone is coming to look at (and maybe
buy) the house,
the dishes needed washing and the bed needed making.
Then the car needed gas and
there was an accident and the road was blocked and
the police have no suggested detours and
I wandered around in unfamiliar neighborhoods, lost -
looking for a way to your house.
So I am late, late, late.
And I'm very, very, hungry…
So let's do lunch, now.

GLENDA KOTCHISH and JANE WILSON

LET'S DO LUNCH

by Jane Ellen Holliday Wilson

I have this friend who was (and really still is) a Rockette. Need I say she is a fascination?

Tall and slender, long flowing natural blond hair (still at 50! Can you imagine?).

You might think the word friend would not apply to such a creature. The word envy, you might say, would lay down a coating so thick that friend couldn't quite get through.

But that is not the case here. She is really quite a treasure.

I met her at a prayer meeting. She was the leader. She called it Centering Prayer. I knew I needed plenty of centering, and Lord knows I needed all the prayer I could get. So, I decided to give it a whirl--and a twirl.

Anyway, she lured me in, introducing me to all of her rambunctious buddies. We prayed, and went on meditative walks, and did Pilates and all kinds of spiritual things like that. The next thing you know, her friends were my friends.

So, the other day that sweet girl threw her own self a birthday party. Here's what the email said, "Anybody who wants to--come celebrate my birthday with me. We'll meet in the parking lot as St. Us at 11:00, drive into town to St. Somebody's and have the Lenten Lunch. (Hopefully they will have the cheese soufflé.) Then we will listen to a good sermon, and come home." Only my Rockette friend could be so self-confident and unassuming as to extend such an invitation. And I wanted to go powerfully bad.

But I couldn't go because, as you can see, it would have

been an all-day affair:

10:30 Drive the 30 minutes from my house to St. Us to meet everybody so we could carpool

11:00 Get there and putter around waiting for everybody else to arrive

11:15 All accounted for; we take off for the 30 minute drive into town

11:45 Finally--get to St. Somebody's

Eat yummy soufflé--yack it up with the girls

12:30 Listen to amazing sermon--always very inspiring

1:15 Chicks once again rounded up--leave for the suburbs

2:00 Finally again--back at St. Us.

2:30 After jabbering and hugging everybody goodbye, leave for the 30 minute drive home

3:00 Back home well fed, well loved, well inspired for Easter, and ready for a nap

And add an hour to the beginning of all of that because those fun girls dress up really funky-cool to go places, and it would take me forever to find the appropriate thing to wear based on the sad state of affairs in my current wardrobe.

There, the whole day is gone.

Besides I had already booked--with no small measure of courage--an appointment that day that would interfere. I was to go look at a house downtown so that, in future, going to the Lenten Lunch would only take an hour and a half, instead of all day. Of course, other conveniences were involved as well, such as not having to get up at 5:00 in the morning to avoid the 8:00 traffic jam into work, and saving lots of gas, and downsizing, and so on.

But I didn't want to tell my whimsical new friend about that appointment just yet.

Because explaining to her why I had an appointment to look at a house meant explaining that I planned to move in the first place. Then I would have to go into all those reasons listed above, plus some. And that was a conversation that we really needed to have over a nice long lunch at a fun place in town--all of which I am happy to do.

But, as we have already established, such a lunch date is going to take all day.

GLENDA KOTCHISH and JANE WILSON

CHAPTER 5 ON THE OTHER HAND

GLENDA KOTCHISH and JANE WILSON

HANDS

Glenda Mace Kotchish

Questions:

1. Her nails, chipped and uneven, a little dirt clinging to the cuticles--what have her hands been doing today?
2. A ring was worn once upon a time, not so long ago, upon her left hand--ring finger. The pale impression remains. Where is the ring now?
3. Her span wide, her fingers not tapered, her knuckles large--is she rough, and her touch--strong and deliberate?
4. Two brown spots above her thumb, veins--large, rising beneath her skin--just how old is she?

Answers:

1. Making clay pots--a messy job.
2. Her ring sits in a dish on her workbench.
3. Throwing a pot--a delicate job, to center, to coax the clay, up--in and out
4. She's old enough to know how.

GLENDA KOTCHISH and JANE WILSON

My Right Hand

Jane Ellen Holliday Wilson

It was supposed to be a meditative exercise—study your right hand for as long as you can without thinking about anything else.

It was designed to give you a break from all the things that go on in your head.

But it turns out my right hand has stories written all over it.

There's the scar on the joint of my pointer finger—the perfectly round piece of flesh that I whittled away, but for enough skin to hold it back in place long enough to heal.

How old was I then? 11? Maybe 12?

We had arrived at the campground at dusk. My sisters and I were in a frenzy to find the best marshmallow roasting sticks, while Momma and Daddy made camp.

I found a great young twig, but, by the time I did, all that was left was the worst of the whittling knives. (Mind you, my mother never owned a decent knife in her life until I bought her one as a grown woman. And these camping knives were all the rejects of her sorrowfully dull collection.)

I was whittling for all I was worth when I just took off the top of that knuckle. First there was the surprise of seeing my skin dangling there. For an instant I thought it an interesting non-event. Then came the slow seeping up of burgundy rivulets of blood; and finally the fiery, throbbing announcement of pain.

I remember being so brave in the midst of it all—it hurt like the dickens, but I was determined not to be a "chicken liver" as my big sisters would have called me had I cried. Nor had I any intention of missing out on those roasted marshmallows. Daddy bandaged it up, and before you knew it I was there by the campfire with my poorly whittled stick.

Then there's the burn mark on my wrist—stressed out young mother—marriage crumbling all around me—I just wanted to bring an afternoon of cheer into my little girl's' day by making some sweet-smelling, happy faced cookies.

No matter that my hands were shaking as I bent down to pull the cookies from the oven, causing me to graze my wrist on the hot rack—again the brave one, "Oh it's no problem at all, little ones. Let's get some milk and our Peter Rabbit plates and have a celebration."

And, the scar that I love the most of all—the one that actually did require a trip to the emergency room and two tiny stitches.

Finally, the right frog was kissed. I had found my prince—soul of my soul—heart of my heart.

Standing at the kitchen sink, staring out the window, again with knife in hand (this time a sharper than sharp Cutco) I was working at some candle wax left in my good candle holders—it had dripped down on them during a romantic dinner the night before.

As I worked I began to daydream—ah happiness— when suddenly the knife slipped.

The exercise: Study your right hand. Why, it's just my right hand—the right hand of a left-handed person. It should be the perfect dull object upon which to meditate.

CHAPTER 6 LETTERS AND EMAILS

GLENDA KOTCHISH and JANE WILSON

THE GREEN BOX OF STATIONERY

Glenda Mace Kotchish

It only exists in her memory now--the green box of stationery. It was a birthday gift from her father, purchased from Everett Wadley, the stationery store at Southside Plaza. Phoebe remembers her mother and father returning from Friday's weekly grocery shopping. She remembers her mother handing it to her--unwrapped.

"Daddy got this for you for your birthday," her mother says and goes back to unloading the brown paper grocery bags.

"Thank you," Phoebe says and sits down at the kitchen table to examine it.

The box is pale green. She removes the white ribbon that holds it closed and lifts the lid. The paper is pale green with a gold scroll of leaves across the top. The stack is also bound in a white ribbon. The matching envelopes are beneath the paper--in two bundles. She closes the lid and pulls the gold knob that opens the little drawer at the bottom of the box. There are note sheets in this compartment. "It will be a good place to store stamps," Phoebe thinks.

"It's perfect," Phoebe says.

"He thought you'd like it," her mother replies.

"I do." Phoebe says.

"Help me put the groceries away and then take these bags to the barrel to burn," instructs her mother.

The brown paper grocery bags are not kept in the house once unpacked. It is a well-known that roaches come from grocery bags and can easily infect a house. So as a matter of course, the bags are burned in the burn-barrel in the backyard. Her father burns the trash once a week. After the groceries are put away, Phoebe takes the bags to the barrel and tosses them in.

Later in her room, Phoebe takes out a sheet of paper from the box and begins a letter to her grandmother in Charlottesville.

Dear Grandma,

Today is my birthday and Daddy got me a nice box of stationery. This paper is from the box. Daddy knows exactly what to get me.

School has been open 4 weeks now. I love the first days of school, the school supplies and the books. I try to get an old book when I pick mine from the teacher's desk, one that's in really bad shape. That way I can write in the margins and underline things. I know the book won't last another year anyway, so they won't fuss at me for writing in it. Can you believe I'm in the 10th grade now? It's a little better than the 9th grade but not much. I like school, it's just the kids are kind of mean outside of class.

Everybody is okay here. I hope you are well. I hope we can come visit soon.

Love,
Phoebe

Phoebe thinks back to those days of letter writing-- letters written to the church friends who had gone off to college, letters to a boy she'd met at church-camp, letters to Sister Harris, the elderly lady from church who moved to South Boston and had given Phoebe her address. Then there are the letters to Sister Harris's grandson who was in the Navy and lonely--the grandson that proposed through the mail and sent a diamond engagement ring. Phoebe remembers the panic of being engaged. How did this happen? She remembers the letter, a few months later to the grandson, breaking off the engagement and enclosing the ring. Imagine! A diamond ring sent in the mail, in a paper envelope.

She remembers the responses stored in the stationery box, sometimes pictures were enclosed--black and white.

She recalls the stamps stored in the little drawer. They cost only five-cents. Phoebe remembers when States did not have official abbreviations. Florida was Fla., Connecticut was Conn. There were no zip codes, and a letter addressed to Mrs. Ida Jones, Rt. 20, Charlottesville, Vir. would be delivered by the Post Office without fail. It was the time before the invention of the rubber stamp "return to sender, insufficient address."

And now, fifty years later Phoebe opens her desk drawer and withdraws a box of notecards. She picks one her grandson will like and begins to write a note. He's only five and she thinks he would like to get some mail-- addressed just to him.

GLENDA KOTCHISH and JANE WILSON

Every Day She Wrote a Letter

Jane Ellen Holliday Wilson

A woman needs a spot of her own

A place to sit and read
And write
And ponder the world as
She knows it

An altar
If you will

For me it was always
And still remains
My velvety moss green
Sofa

Circa Depression era and
Plenty funky
No matter where it sits

In the elegant lavender living room
Looking out over the
The raising of my sweet girls,
The rising of the sun

Or in the roomy ivory bedroom

Of my single mom house
Three candles and the
Happy Home Buddha tranquilly grinning
From the table close by

Or as it is now
In this crisp aqua townhouse living room
Where my husband and I are attempting to be
Fashionable downsizers

I am still drawn to my comfy
Perch

Across from it sits my mother's
Rocker
The one that taught me all about
Altars in the first place

Abandoned now because
She can no longer get
Up and out of it
I snatched it up for myself
Understanding full well
Its intrinsic worthiness

~~~

Once
Long ago
It was an altar *par excellence*

When Momma ascended
Her rocking chair throne

MAKE NO ASSUMPTIONS

It was as if a holy cloud surrounded
Her

Sometimes a cloud of
Sacred authority
As when she held court on
Saturday night

Three girls fresh from the tub
Sitting on the sofa across
From her
Laurence Welk just tuning
Up his orchestra

One by one we were
Summoned for the
Solemn pin curling
Ceremony

Performed to insure that
Every hair would be in place
For Sunday School the next morning

The hair of my sisters'
Generally complied
But oh not mine
By church service curls
Would be revolting
Shamefully

It was the cloud of

Divine silence
That fascinated me most

No way in this world that
Any one of us could get
Very far from anyone else
In that tiny
Ranch style home

Yet Momma could disappear
When she took to
That chair

It was where she
Graded first grade papers
Late into the night

Where she studied her own
Sunday School lesson
Read her *Book-of-the-Month Club*
Books

And the thing I remember best
Was this:

Every day she wrote a letter

I was the youngest
The last to leave home
So I knew this
In a way others didn't

MAKE NO ASSUMPTIONS

I had more time on my hands
And few people to watch.
Momma's habits became
Very clear to me

At first it was just
One letter to *her* mother

Then it became
One to her mother--
Next day
One to my sister
Away at college

A year later
One to her mother--
Next day
One to my sister
Away at college--
Next day
One to my other sister
Also, away at college

And then she began again

(The stationery began to get less
Extravagant as the tuitions mounted)

She would be writing them
When I got up in the morning
Before making breakfast
Before her long day at school

There she sat in the sturdy
Rocker by the window
Balancing paper and pen
On her generous lap

It wasn't long until
I was off at school
And incorporated
Into the warp and the weft
Of these letters traveling
Through the mountains

I could count the days by
Her letters
Every fourth day now
I received her attention

And sure enough, on my end
Every fourth day a letter appeared
Eliciting the vision of
Momma sitting in that chair

They would be short and sweet
A page or two, maybe three

Nothing special:
Things that worried her
People she had seen
Places she and Daddy had been
When they would be up
For the next football game

MAKE NO ASSUMPTIONS

As with the wild curly hair on my little girl head
I was a bit more rambunctious
Than my sisters

Thus my letters surely
Carried more
Admonitions from Richmond
And up those hills
To VA Tech

But always those letters
Were signed
Love, Momma
In the end

Teaching me that

A woman needs a place of her own

A place to sit and read
And write
And ponder the world as
She knows it

An altar
If you will

GLENDA KOTCHISH and JANE WILSON

A Box of Letters

by Glenda Mace Kotchish

Phoebe and Mel walk into Phoebe's mother's house. The front door is never locked. When the house was bought, the key was handed over and then misplaced.

There are three possible ways to go; straight ahead leads upstairs; to the right is the dining room--turned into den which has been painted a dark green; to the left is the living room with French provincial furniture, a gold and green carpet on hardwood floors. This room is used only at Christmas and on the rare occasions when there are guests.

"Mama? Anyone here?" Phoebe calls out as she closes the door behind them. No one answers.

"Let's check the kitchen," Phoebe says.

They walk through the den and into the kitchen, Phoebe leading the way. Mildred, Phoebe's mother is looking into the refrigerator. When she closes the door with a half-eaten cherry pie in her hand, she sees Phoebe and drops the dish.

"Oh my, you scared me" she says. "Look what you made me do." She sees Mel and smiles. "Well hello there."

"Let me help," Phoebe says as she stoops to pick up the broken dish.

"No, go get the broom," Mildred says.

Phoebe goes to the screened-in-porch, gets the broom and dustpan and comes back into the kitchen to find Mildred holding a piece of the glass dish in her hand. Her hand is bleeding.

"You've cut yourself," Phoebe says.

Mildred grunts and walks to the kitchen sink. She turns on the water and holds her bleeding hand under the flow.

Phoebe sweeps up the broken dish and pie and tosses them into the trashcan. She hangs the broom and dustpan on the hook on the porch and comes back into the kitchen to find Mel and her mother laughing.

"What's so funny?" she says, smiling herself.

"Your Mom was telling me about the first cherry pie she made," Mel laughs.

"I didn't know to take the seeds out of the cherries and your Dad would take a bite and then spit out the seeds," Mildred chuckles as she wraps a paper towel on the cut.

"I remember that story," says Phoebe. "Do you want a band aide?"

"No, it's fine. It's stopped bleeding."

"So, why did you want me to come over today?" asks Phoebe.

"I moved the last of your stuff out of the house last week and put it in the shed. That's all."

"What did I forget?"

"A bunch of books, your easel and a box of pictures and stuff. I went through it all and kept anything I wanted," Mildred replies.

"What do you mean? You kept what you wanted? What did you take, exactly?" asks Phoebe frowning.

"Some pictures of your brothers and your Dad," Mildred says as she looks in the refrigerator again.

"But that was my stuff," Phoebe objects. She puts her hands on her hips.

"What's in my house is mine," Mildred announces as she pulls a dish of cobbler from the refrigerator and closes the door. "Want some cobbler, Mel?"

"Sure. What kind?" Mel asks.

"Peach. I'll heat it up for you. I have ice cream too. Would you like some on your cobbler?"

"You bet," says Mel.

"Phoebe, how about you?" Mildred asks.

"No thanks. I'm going out to the shed." Phoebe heads for the back door.

"I'll come with you, Phoebe," volunteers Mel as he rises from the table.

"Ok," Phoebe says.

"Your cobbler will be ready when you get back. Don't take long," Mildred calls after them.

The shed is brick and matches the two-story colonial house. It has no electricity. The sunlight from the one window catches the flecks of dust as Phoebe opens the door and steps inside.

"It's a little musty in here" says Mel as he looks around picking up tools and putting them down.

"Here's my stuff," says Phoebe walking over to a corner of the shed where an easel has been propped against a cardboard box.

"My sister bought me this easel for Christmas one year," remarks Phoebe as she moves it aside and opens the cardboard box. Inside she finds four books of poetry, two high-school yearbooks, some sketchbooks and another box. She thumbs through the sketchbooks remembering the high school art classes--the assignment was 20 sketches every six weeks. She thinks that if the sketch books had been pocket size it would have been a lot easier to sketch on the go. These large books are overwhelming--big, blank, white pages staring up at you begging for a picture. She sets the books aside and opens the smaller box. Inside are bundles of letters bound together with rubber bands, and stacks of pictures.

Phoebe looks up to see Mel still inspecting the tools and playing with the vice grip that is mounted on her father's workbench.

She picks up a pack of letters and unbinds them--her high school pen pal. Pierre was from France. She always wondered why the Spanish teacher gave her a French pen pal. Maybe they ran out of Spanish speaking pen pals. Pierre had sent a picture of himself. In the photograph he has a very large nose and does not smile.

Phoebe unbinds the next pack of letters--from her

friend Gracie. Gracie attended the same church as Phoebe's family and was in the youth group. Gracie was five years her senior. Phoebe remembers the friendship that was somewhat of a mystery to her. Why was Gracie so nice to her when she was ostracized by everyone else? Gracie wrote her from college and sent pictures. Here's one of her in the Glee Club. When did she find time to write me? Phoebe wonders. And why? Phoebe looks at the pictures of Gracie, each year a little more mature, a little more worldly, a little less churchy.

The next pack is in air-mail envelopes, military--the navy from the FPO (Fleet Post Office). Phoebe remembers these well. They are so official looking "FPO" and from the sailor, Scott. Phoebe opens a letter and scans it.

"We are in port. Some of the guys are going to Disneyland so I'm going along. We have a little shore leave and can hitch a ride to Anaheim pretty easy…"

There are stacks of these letters. Phoebe opens several more. The letters become more personal, they speak of love--each a little more ardent than the last. Phoebe wonders "When did it take that path to announcements of love? We didn't even know each other except on paper." And when it came time for leave and a trip home, Phoebe remembers that awkward meeting when they realized they had nothing to say--in person.

Phoebe looks through the stack of pictures--none of the two of them--only Scott. Scott on ship, Scott in his whites, Scott in his dress blues, Scott working on an airplane on ship. Scott with his shirt off, on deck.

Mel wanders over to where Phoebe is seated. "What do you have there?"

"Some old letters and pictures I've saved."

"Oh, so this is Scott. Mind if I take a look?" Mel reaches out for the pictures.

Phoebe hands over the pictures and watches him examine each one. His brow creases. His lips purse a little. Ever so often he lets out a little grunt of disapproval. "He's a little on the skinny side, don't you think?" Mel remarks.

"Oh, not so much," Phoebe say.

"What's with the mustache? I thought these sailors had to be squeaky clean."

"I don't know. I guess they have a little latitude," Phoebe responds.

"What was his rank anyway?"

"Gosh, I don't know, probably entry level--whatever that is," Phoebe says as she stands and starts to reload the box of letters and pictures.

As she reaches for the pictures in Mel's hand, he withdraws them out of her reach.

"Since we're engaged, there's no need for you to be hanging on to these," Mel says as he holds the pictures above her head.

"Really?" Phoebe asks. "It is part of my life--knowing Scott."

"It's over right?" asks Mel.

"Of course. You know that. It was a long time ago."

Although Phoebe doesn't care about the letters, something registers off kilter about Mel's suggestion to toss them.

"Good. Then you'll have no problem with putting them in the trash, or shredder if you prefer," say Mel. "Which is it, trash or shredder?" He thumbs through the stack and drops some on the floor.

Phoebe stoops to retrieve them at the same time as Mel. Their heads bump and both are surprised.

"Ouch," says Phoebe as she scoops up the letters and rubs her head.

Mel takes them from her hand. "I'll toss these for you." He opens the shed door, and as he leaves, Herbie, the family dog, bounds in and wags his tail enthusiastically at Phoebe.

"Hello old boy. How have you been?" Phoebe

scratches his ears and Herbie thumps his tail. He opens his mouth in a little smile.

"You need a brushing, don't you boy. Where is your brush?" Phoebe looks around the shed and finds Herbie's brush, leash and assorted balls on a shelf. She gets the brush and sits on the floor and begins grooming the dog.

"So when was the last time anyone did this for you? You have some mighty tangles here. I might need the scissors," Phoebe remarks.

She continues to brush the dog and rubs her sore head from time to time. Some leaves blow in the open door. "Soon it will be winter," Phoebe says, "The leaves will be off the trees – and then Thanksgiving and then a wedding," she tells Herbie. Herbie rolls on his back and holds up his legs for more brushing.

"You're very submissive old friend. But you *are* getting exactly what you want aren't you?"

Finally Phoebe finishes. "You look mighty smart Herbie. Would you like a treat? I hear there is cobbler in the kitchen."

Phoebe turns and picks up her box and her easel. "That was some head knocking," she tells Herbie who sits regarding her--waiting for the treat.

"I don't care about the letters, really. But… but what?" Phoebe asks herself.

She closes the shed door and she and Herbie... together walk into the house. She hears Mel and her mother laughing.

"But… but… butting heads." Phoebe closes her eyes before opening the door, takes a deep breath. There are things to be done and things to be undone she whispers.

Before Email

For my friend Susan

Jane Ellen Holliday Wilson

Before email, we sent letters, trunks full of letters. It was in one such trunk of my mother's that I found the answer to the family riddle of why she kept that framed envelope hanging above her dressing table all those years. The one she always told us was there because she just really liked the stationary, and once she got the room painted, she realized it was the same color as her walls--elegant pale grey linen. Her bedspread matched the envelope's navy trim. So she just decided to frame it, and hang it there where she put on her face every day. The envelope was totally blank, but it had fold-marks as though it had been tucked inside some other mailing. Mom always said, "I know it's odd, but then I'm a little odd myself, so there."

I was in no way prepared for the answer--a life-changing one--that *answered* so many things. Even now, years after that lid opened on the trunk, I can't quite square my feelings about finally learning the secrets that old trunk contained; secrets that caused me to ask so many other questions about myself, the adults who raised me, and didn't; and about the toll extracted by love and sacrifice.

My mother was a *different* woman, to say the least. Cold to the touch, and to the core it seemed--especially to me. I had always believed this. I can remember reaching up to grab her hand as a young child, and feeling her recoil. All of us tiptoed around her. Sweet Daddy made up for it though, with candy in pockets and a big hug for each and every one of us when he got home from work. It had been 30 years now since Daddy had left us. His affection sorely missed since that summer he died suddenly of a heart attack at 55.

So this awakening began after Mom's funeral, as my five siblings and I collected on the sofa in her living room telling tales and looking over old pictures. My sister said, "Anna, we all know she was hardest on you for some reason."

This was the first time anyone had actually acknowledged what I had always felt in my heart, but never allowed myself to speak. I found the verbal aroma of these words sinking into my soul as though I had just been presented with a burned up pot roast for my birthday dinner, with no apologies, mind you.

I said nothing at the time. When I was sure that the conversation had drifted off in another direction, I carefully wiped the small line of tears rolling down each cheek, hoping no one noticed my contorted complexity of emotions.

The next day, the six of us set about the house diving into the packing up and disposing of 60 years of my mother's adult life. I was assigned the back half of the attic. My sister, Sarah took the front. We quickly created a trash heap of moth eaten clothes, financial papers dating to the 40's, including paid off charges at Harris's Grocery (Mr. Harris long dead now), Dr. Anderson's charges for removing all our tonsils, Mom's receipt from the decorating store for her bedroom (paint chip and fabric sample attached), Daddy's receipt for the purchase of that old fishing boat he named *My Reward*, and so on. It was about noon when I arrived at the trunk.

"Sarah, remember this old trunk?" I shouted from over by the far southern window.

"Of course, it's *the trunk*; the one that has *always* been off limits--locked tight just in case anyone dared try to open it; the one that Mom refused to open, no matter what," Sarah replied.

"I know. Remember the time curiosity got the best of me? We were up here playing *Little Women* and I got to messing with the thing. I just wanted into it something awful. Mom came up to get us for dinner and caught me….," I mused.

"….And boy did she ever tan your hide," finished Sarah. "Not a one of us was going anywhere near that thing after that."

"Don't you think it's a little strange that she left it here," I asked my sister. "If it's contents were all that big a secret, you'd think she would have gotten rid of it."

Sarah agreed, "She had plenty of warning that the end was coming. She could have gotten it out of here without us ever even knowing. It would have been easy enough. Who were those people she hired to haul away all that stuff? You know, the good stuff."

I thought for a moment, "Oh you mean those college guys--*Brains and Brawn*--she loved that. When I was here with her after the first tumor surgery I watched as they hauled away all of our old dress-ups and dolls and that beautiful vase from Grandmama Sally. I wanted to scream, but how can you argue with a cancer patient?"

"Well maybe she wanted someone to find out what was inside *after she died*. Maybe it has some great family treasure in there that's worth millions," quipped Sarah. "She can't tan your hide now. I say go for it. I think it's time. And after the price you paid for your curiosity, I think you deserve to be the one to find any *treasure* that might be inside."

That was all I needed--a bit of a dare. I went down to the basement, got myself a hammer, a big screwdriver and even a crowbar, and I went at the thing while everybody else wandered off to the kitchen for lunch. I just couldn't help myself. I had to know.

It was easier to get into that I had expected. Now that Mom's magic *fear powers* had been dissipated in the known world, I found that all it took was a little prying here and there and I was in.

When the lid opened I felt the strangest sensation. It was almost as if Mom was there with me, but in a good way--a way I certainly had never known in life. There was this strange sense of wonder.

Inside--no golden family heirloom that would allow us all to quit our jobs, not even elegant antique evening gowns--only letters--bunches of letters. Disappointed, I pulled up a large trash bag and went to work--plenty enough were bound for the bin--boring accounts of daily life from our Aunt Caroline, notes sent back and forth between girlfriends in elementary school. I saved one or two to share with the family downstairs.

Then I found them--three large bundles tied up in satin ribbons (unusually romantic for our mother who was not given to flights of fancy). Most interesting of all were the envelopes. I recognized them immediately. The stationary was exactly like the blank envelope hanging above her dressing table--elegant pale grey linen and edged with navy.

These envelopes were not blank though (like the one we had looked at for years). Her maiden name--Elizabeth Anne Winston, along with the address of the house she grew up in--was typed in crisp Times New Roman on many of them, meaning that they had been coming since before her marriage to Daddy. I noticed that they were addressed this way regardless of when they were sent though (before Daddy or after Daddy). No hint from the outside as to the sender. Hum. Maybe there was more to this, "I really like the stationery," business than met the eye.

I began opening the letters:

Dear Bess,
How I miss you. This war is hell, hell I tell you....I don't know how to express my love for you
Andy

I was hooked. The letters went on and on. I sat for hours and hours reading them. When my siblings finally came looking for me, I was still there, tears--now unchecked--streaming down my face.

When they asked me what on earth was the matter, I gave them the shortest answer I could manage; "Mom was in love once--not with Daddy, before him. To a man named Andy. He left for the war before they could get married. By the time he came home she had married Daddy.

"Daddy knew she was in love with someone else, and he married Mom anyway. I think he must really *have* loved her. He married her anyway and he married her fast because... because she was already pregnant with me....

....Here's a picture." I looked down at my hands and found that I was clutching this picture tight to my chest. So tight in fact that it took me a minute to unclasp it. I felt the blood rush back into my hands when I let it go.

I passed it to Maxine, my baby sister first. "Oh my God, it's him," she gasped.

"Who?" The others exclaimed.

"You know that guy we were wondering about at the funeral? The one we had never seen before? The guy hovering around the edges? I sighed, "It was him. My own father, and I didn't even know it."

"Anyhow, when Andy came home it didn't take him long to figure out why she had married Daddy so fast. After all it wasn't easy to be a single mom in those days-- the stigma would have been overwhelming. He sent her one final letter asking her to leave Daddy and come live with him. He sent that envelope (you know, the one hanging on her wall) folded inside. He told her if he opened his mailbox and found it there, he would know she was coming. If not he would understand," I explained. "He said he loved her no matter what, and he loved his sweet baby Anna too," I sobbed, burying my face in my hands.

My family let me cry. Wrapping me in their love. Eventually I realized that each one of my siblings was touching me gently--on an arm, a knee, a shoulder. Sarah was patting my hair. Their assurance that I was still one of them was palpable, and much coveted at that moment.

So now we know. Mom chose Daddy and all of us instead of Andy. (By the time Andy made it home from the war, Sarah and Jonathan (twins) had already been born. The others would come along well after Andy had written that final letter. Even after Daddy died, she didn't waver in that choice.

But she painted her room to match the envelope and the decision she made (not the other way around as she had always told us). Leaving me with more fathers, and perhaps more love than I ever knew I had, but definitely more questions than answers. The first among them-- would I ever get the nerve to track down that *strange man at the funeral*, look him in the eyes, eyes that might very well be mine, and ask him if he was in fact, my father?

CHAPTER 7 HERO STORIES

GLENDA KOTCHISH and JANE WILSON

About Jack

by Glenda Mace Kotchish

Jack wasn't brilliant. He wasn't really smart either. That's what they'd told him in guidance--anyway. He'd given up on school and had only a ninth grade education. It had taken him eleven years to get that, not counting summer schools. His father wanted him to finish high school. His mother didn't care.

He looked like his father: short, straight dark hair, dark brown eyes and strong. But he had his mother's disposition--lazy, and her aspirations--none. He did however want a jeep, so he got a job in the tobacco company factory, sweeping up debris from the machines. He worked nights--four nights on and three nights off. They gave him free cigarettes, a carton a week. They paid all of his insurance premium, and he got two weeks vacation a year--to start. If he stayed on board, after five years, he would get three weeks vacation; and for every five years thereafter, another week--up to six weeks max. He had a job for life--if he wanted it.

His hobbies were camping, hunting and smoking weed. He lived at home with his parents--over the garage. His father made him pay rent. But Jack always ran short on cash and borrowed the rent money back from his mother, almost every week.

On Jack's twenty-first birthday, three things happened. First, his friends took him to a strip joint and he got totally drunk and high from some smack (the smack--a birthday present from his friend, Charlie).

Secondly, when Charlie dropped him off at home at 3 a.m., Jack dropped his keys somewhere between the driveway and the stairs to the apartment door. His father, hearing a commotion in the front yard, turned on the floodlights to discover his son, stark naked, yelling, "Let me in old man," to which his father took *exception*, and after unlocking the garage apartment, informed his son that by noon the next day, he'd better have moved out of the garage or he'd find his stuff on the curb.

And the third thing that happened was, Jack took *exception* to his father's attitude, threw on some jeans and a shirt--found his stash of weed, located his lost keys, and got in his jeep and drove off into the night--destination the hunt club--ninety miles into the hills. He'd have made it, had it not been for the deer standing in the road. Jack veered to the left to miss her. He hit a rut and flipped the jeep into a ravine.

Great Bear, asleep in the tree sniffs the air--the scent of man, and man's shell filling her nostrils. It is clearly man's shell--hard, sometimes cold, sometimes hot, loud and roaring. And when silent--man always emerges. She smells him before she hears him and then she sees him. She also sees Deer silently nibbling at the wildflowers near man's trail. Deer hears man's shell, sprints into trail, and when the light strikes her eyes, she is blinded and stands still. Man's shell jumps off his trail and rolls through the grasses down into the ravine. Deer flees into the forest. As always, man appears from his shell but this time not on his two legs. He is flying through the air. When he lands, man is very still. Great Bear is curious and backs down her tree. She has no cubs. Cougar stole both cubs from her last litter.

Great Bear walks a wide circle around man. She sees that he has no stick with fire. He is very still, but he breathes. He makes no sound. She approaches closer until she is standing over him. Man's eyes are closed. She sits down beside him and watches. Man only breathes. She has seen his kind before--a memory, not her own, yet one she owns none the less--dark skin, dark straight hair, short in stature, yet strong. She waits for the memory to become clearer. Something doesn't belong. She waits. She remembers. The smell from his breath is different. This sour smell does not belong to the memory of his kind. She waits and watches.

Soon it will be dawn. She thinks of her cubs and of Cougar. She mourns for her cubs. She is lonely. Cougar will come and the man will be no more. She trots to man's shell and sniffs. Bad smells are coming from man's shell and spilling onto the grass. She pulls man's things from his shell. She has seen man's things before when she has come upon his camps. They sleep in dens they bring with them and soft furs they slip in and out of. They always have their fire and sticks and food. Sometimes they eat the fish from the stream. She finds man's sleeping fur and takes it to him. She nudges man onto his fur. She pulls and pushes until man is on his sleeping fur. Cougar will be here soon. She drags man and his fur through the forest to her last den, one she has dug below the roots of a large oak, near a stream. She pulls man into her den. He is safe from Cougar. He will live.

Jack opens his eyes a sliver. It is pitch dark. He thinks, "I'm dead." He panics and tries to raise his head. The pain is piercing and he lays it back down. He moves his fingers and feels something soft under him, cool--silky, nylon. He slowly moves his arms, and then his feet and legs. Pain shoots up his left leg. He stills himself. He passes out.

Great Bear alternates sleeping in the oak tree and in the den. She forages the forest and meadow for berries and nuts. She fishes the stream. She guards the den. Cougar does not come. Man sleeps; he moves but makes no sounds. It is good. She leaves berries beside him which he does not eat. Many days have past. Man must eat soon.

Jack slips in and out of consciousness. His mouth is dry. Light filters in through a space. His hand touches some things--small, soft and roundish. He cups a few in his hand and then holds them in front of his face. Blackberries. He slips them in his mouth and his juices flow. He eats all that are there, then falls back to sleep.

He dreams. He is in his jeep, on a road, graveled. Although it is daytime he cannot see out of his windshield. He is driving blindly. "How can this be," he thinks. He blinks his eyes but there is only darkness. He continues driving and comes to a bridge. Water is rising. He needs to cross the bridge but he is afraid. The water in the river is churning.

He awakens. It is dark--pitch black. He feels a presence beside him--a very large presence. He hears breathing. He is afraid. His fear paralyzes him. He is silent, too afraid to scream out in his pain and fear. The night passes. He sees a soft shaft of light. He hears movement. The light is momentarily blocked. He is alone. He moans. Despite his fear, he is exhausted and falls asleep. Dreams overtake him once again.

Great Bear drinks from the spring. It is time for man to drink. She enters the den. She nudges man. She grunts at him to rouse him. She knows he has not slept throughout the night. She could feel his fear of her in the dark. She lays down beside him and watches. Light filters in through the den opening.

Jack dreams. He dreams that he is in a city--a familiar street. He is driving his jeep but he is in the back seat. The jeep is all white. He is coming to a crossroad, a busy intersection--Main Street. It is snowing. The light is very bright. He cannot see for the snow and the light. There are figures, a man and a woman, holding a baby. They are dressed in white. They cannot see him, nor he them. He is afraid that he will hit them with his jeep. He enters the intersection. His jeep veers right. He opens his eyes and sees Great Bear.

Great Bear speaks in a low, purring voice to soothe him. As she continues to purr, man's fear subsides. She is very still except for her purring.

Man is calm.

Great Bear tugs at man's sleeping fur and pulls him toward the den's opening. Man moans but uses his arms and right leg to scoot along the den floor as Great Bear pulls him into the sunshine. They are working together now.

Exhausted from this small effort, Jack breathes the fresh air into his lungs as he lies on his stomach just outside the den. The morning is cool and he feels the dew from the grass on his face. He rolls to his side and sits up feeling light headed. He sees the stream. His thirst is all consuming. He looks at his arms. They are covered in contusions. He feels his left leg knowing before touching it that it is broken. He is barefoot except for his socks. He rolls up his jeans on his left leg and is thankful that there is no bone protruding from his skin. But clearly, a bone is broken in his calf somewhere. He breaks down and weeps.

Great Bear watches man from a distance and then turns and walks into the forest to search for food.

Jack slowly and painfully drags himself to the spring where he drinks greedily and then vomits. He rinses his face and tries to drink again, this time taking small sips from his cupped hand. His stomach growls but accepts the fluid. Feeling weak, Jack lies on his back alongside the stream and looks up into the trees at the blue sky and sunshine.

He thinks. "How did I come to be in a bear's den? Why has the bear not killed me? How long have I been here? Just where is--here? He remembers his jeep, the deer. He remembers his father. "I am alone," he thinks. "I am alone and hopelessly lost. The bear should have killed me, as I will die soon anyway."

Jack drinks from the spring again. Sitting up he sees the bear, fifty or so feet away, watching him. Jack looks at her, unafraid. She lowers her head onto her front paws and continues to watch.

"What?" Jack asks.

"What now?" he asks again. The bear yawns.

Jack yawns in response.

The bear slowly gets up and lumbers towards Jack.

Jack freezes. His fear returns. "She has been saving me for now," he thinks. "This is it. Death. I am about to die."

He closes his eyes and trembles, waiting to be mauled. He hears a splash and opens his eyes. Upstream the bear is in the creek, looking down into the water. Jack watches her stand there, still, patiently waiting. And then he sees her thrust her paw into the stream and bring up a fish. She holds it in her mouth and walks downstream toward him. She tosses it at his feet, turns and disappears into the forest.

Jack is astounded. He figures out how to eat the fish by using a stone from the stream to open it and get to the meat. He rinses the meat in the stream and eats it raw--slowly.

After eating he thinks, "I am useless--worse than useless. A bear is taking care of me, dammit."

He crawls back to the den where he finds berries laid out. He eats them. He pulls his sleeping bag back into the den and goes to sleep. When he wakes, it is night and he is alone. He thinks, "Where is the bear?" He lays awake, and for the first time in his life--truly thinks.

Great Bear does not return to the den that night, or the next day. At first light, on the second day, Jack crawls from the den. He drags his sleeping bag behind him and tears off strips of cloth. He crawls to the spring and drinks his fill. He searches until he finds some branches that he uses as splints. He binds them on his leg with the strips of cloth. This done, using another branch as a walking stick, he rises to his feet and, following the steam east, starts toward home, his tattered sleeping bag strapped to his back.

GLENDA KOTCHISH and JANE WILSON

Alberto

by Jane Ellen Holliday Wilson

His first memory was of the sun rising over the sharp, yet succulent green mountains; the aroma of his grandmother's beans and rice already scenting the cool morning air; his papa calling, "Alberto, little man, stop your daydreaming and come to breakfast. The day will be long and we must get to it."

Indeed the days were long in their tiny Guatemalan village. The men worked the fields and cared for the livestock from dawn until dusk, while the women tended the fires, cooking and cleaning, weaving fabric for rugs and clothing and looking after the children. It was a simple, wholesome life.

Until a dark cloud began to fall over the land. By the age of six, Alberto began to hear the men talking of something called *pandilla*. They were being reported in villages down in the valley. The men seemed troubled as they talked.

On the way home from the fields Alberto asked, "Papa, what is a gang? Is it a wild animal, a beast?"

His papa paused and thought for a moment. "Yes Alberto, the gangs are much like packs of wild animals. But they are men—desperate men unable to find meaningful work in their towns. They turn to drugs and evildoing to get by. They come to other villages and force their way of life upon the people. But, my son, you mustn't worry. I will protect you and Mama and your sisters. I will keep us safe."

But word of the gangs continued among the men. It seemed they were growing closer and closer to Alberto's village. Despite his father's promise of protection, Alberto could tell that all the villagers were growing fearful. His best friend Pablo had left in the middle of the night with his parents.

"Where did he go, Papa?"

"To America, my son. They say there is hope for a good life there."

"Will we go to America, Papa?"

"Indeed we may someday, Alberto."

"But Papa, I don't want to leave the mountain and the sunrise. And how will we take Grandmama? She is so old."

"Grandmama will stay. The gangs have no interest in old women."

"Oh Papa, how can we live without Grandmama to love us?"

"She will love us still my son, no matter where we are." Papa said this with a smile on his face, but Alberto could clearly see sorrow in his eyes.

Alberto was not happy about this at all. He grew more and more troubled by the prospect of leaving his home. He tried hard to enjoy each sunrise, fearing it might be his last.

And finally, the day came. It was just two weeks before Alberto's eighth birthday. Papa came to him at his bed, early in the morning and said, "Wake up little man. Today is the day that we make our way to America."

"No, Papa, no! Please don't make us go!"

"I am sorry little man, but we must. Now hop up and be brave. Put on a good face for you mother and sisters. These are the hard things of life and we must show courage."

Alberto tried to be brave, but tears ran down his cheeks when it came time to hug Grandmama goodbye. He saw tears in her eyes as well.

Grandmama reach down gently and folded him in her arms. She held him tight and said, "Now remember, my precious, when you see the morning sunrise, or the twinkling stars of the night, remember that you and I—we are still under the same big sky. I will never leave you, or forget you. I will love you forever."

It was a comforting thought—one that come to him often in the years to come.

The journey was arduous—over land and sea. Their feet were blistered, their shoes worn. Mamma was often seasick and Alberto's sisters cried a lot. Alberto had long passed his eighth birthday by the time they made it across the border to America and begun to trek their way up the East Coast.

He found it an ugly place—no mountains anywhere, just dirty, frightening cities. Most people did not speak his language. And when they found someone who did, they often lived in squalor.

"Papa, why have you brought us here? There are no mountains, no beautiful sunrise, no one who knows our name."

"Patience my son, we will find our way. And you will grow fond of your new home in time."

They worked their way up the coast—his mother taking in laundry and sewing, his father picking up odd jobs as painter, gardener, kitchen help in short-order restaurants. One day they arrived in South Richmond, Virginia, along a road called Jefferson Davis Highway. ("Jeff Davis," he soon learned that people called it—and not necessarily in a nice tone of voice.)

It seemed that there were many people of Latin descent there, though. They had gathered from countries all over South America. Their dialects were often different, but at least Alberto could understand them. It was good to hear his native tongue once again.

Papa told him, "They tell us there is a kind priest here at the Catholic Church. He is not a Latino, like us, but they say he speaks our language very well. He will help us find work, and schools and a doctor for your mamma now that she is expecting another baby—let's hope for a boy this time."

It was not a pretty place, and Alberto did not feel very safe there at first, but after two long years of wandering, he was anxious to learn to be a real American. Father Thomas indeed turned out to be a kindhearted and helpful person. He went with his mother to enroll him and his sisters in school.

The *Good Father* bounded into the school as though he were a child himself, "Good morning keepers of academia, I have brought you another set of young scholars to train up and make you proud of your accomplishments and theirs," the jolly priest bellowed as he usher an uneasy Alberto and his sisters through the door of the principal's office. The man truly had a way of chasing away the tensions of life.

There were English classes at the parish, and Alberto was enrolled in those as well. He learned softball—very similar to a game he had played back home. He learned quickly and became a strong student and star athlete.

Now that the family was settled, there was more food on the table. Papa had found a steady job with a large landscaping company, and Mamma, after the birth of his baby brother, had begun working for a seamstress in a place called Carytown. It was a place full of elegant shops and wealthy ladies who always seemed to have balls to attend. Mamma had plenty of work. Often she brought her sewing home.

And home was getting better day-by-day. At first they had shared a trailer with two other families. Then, for a time, they lived in a rundown old motel room. Now they had a little apartment with a nice yard. It was owned by a kind lady who ran an art gallery. She lived next door and tried her best to help them. She would bring the girls little treats, and even managed to dig up an old softball mitt that had belonged to her now grown son. Did she know that without it, Alberto would not have been able to go out for the team?

Even so, it wasn't all fun and games for Alberto. It was not long before he learned that there was a fierce rivalry between the African Americans and the Latinos. Never enough *turf* to go around it seemed—or anything else for that matter. The struggling African Americans felt that the Latinos were moving in on their territory. They made it hard for Alberto and his friends. There were fights and bullying, and Alberto's family quickly discovered that there were plenty of drugs around too.

One day Alberto came home with a black eye. His mother sighed deeply, "Alberto, what has happened to you?"

"Mamma, it was not my fault. On the way home from school I stopped in the store to buy an apple for me, and some for the girls. I had some change. Not much, just a dollar and fifty cents. But there were some thugs behind me who saw me put the money in my pocket. They waited until I was away from the store, and then they jumped me, and took my money. At least they didn't take the apples. None of them care much for apples."

That night Alberto's father said, "Son, you must watch your back--wise as a fox and gentle as a lamb. You must focus on your school work, and your sports and stay as far as you can from those bad boys."

"I do my best Papa, but you don't know how hard it is." It was hard indeed, but Alberto applied himself to his studies and to his sport—baseball now. Time passed, and Alberto's English became admirable. He was good at math and the sciences, especially biology. He began to dream of graduating and becoming a U.S. citizen, even of going to college someday.

His teachers and coaches helped him along the way and by sixteen things were looking bright. Mamma had started her own seamstress shop and had two employees of her own, and Papa had progressed up the chain to crew manager at the landscape company. Grandmama had even come to visit a time or two over the years.

It was late March of Alberto's junior year that he saw Father Thomas standing outside his history class door. This time the kindly priest held no look of mischief on his face. In fact, his brow was a bit creased, and looked as though some sadness had come over him. Alberto wondered why he was there, but didn't give it much thought. Father Thomas could often be seen in the halls. The bell rang. Alberto made his way into the hall.

Father Thomas tapped him on the shoulder, "Alberto, it's your papa."

"What is it, Father Thomas? What is it about Papa?"

"I'm afraid there has been an accident Alberto. Come with me. Your mother needs you at the hospital."

A lawn mower had flipped, pinning Papa under it for some time. His leg was broken severely, and nerves in his arm had been severed.

After a long operation to repair what he could, the doctor came to the door of the waiting room to tell the family that Papa would walk again someday, but he would use a cane for the rest of his life. And his arm would never be the same. And it would be months, maybe years before he could return to work.

The doctor looked around the room. "Are you Alberto?"

"Yes sir, I am."

"He is asking for you, son. You had better go and speak with him before the others."

"Yes sir."

Alberto, head hanging, trudged off to the intensive care unit. There was Papa looking pale and weak. Alberto had never seen his father this way. Something in his gut turned over—a nagging sense that nothing would ever be the same.

Bravely, Alberto took Papa's hand and looked into his eyes. There were tears there—not just the sad look Alberto had seen so many years ago when they left

Guatemala, but real tears--tears of desperation--running down his father's cheeks. This was something he had never seen before.

"I am so, so sorry son. I have failed you. I am afraid the work will fall on your shoulders now. We will have to find a job for you." The tears spilled over into a deep guttural weeping, "I have ruined your dreams. I have let my family down!"

"Papa you mustn't. Please stop this crying. You are too weak for it. This was not your fault. It was a terrible accident. I will help. We will find a way to make ends meet. No worries. Please no worries." Alberto patted his father's hand, and brushed away his tears, but deep down, in his own soul, he knew his father was right. His dreams were up-ended.

As he walked to school the next day he found himself lost in his head. All he could think about was his father's pay. How on earth would he replace it? All through the day he thought about it. When the final bell rang, he realized that he had no idea what his school assignments were. In fact, he couldn't even remember being in class. What on earth was he going to do?

"Hey Alberto, I hear your dad had an accident." He heard the words coming from Torrez. Torrez had never spoken to Alberto before, and that was just fine. The guy was well known to be head of one of the drug gangs that hung out on the corner by the baseball field. Alberto always steered clear of them as he made his way to the locker rooms, but today he had not been paying attention. Still it was odd to hear this hoodlum call is name. Alberto had no idea Torrez even knew who he was. It must be the nature of his business to know these things about people—theirs loves, their needs, their weaknesses.

"Alberto, my friend. So sorry to hear of this tragedy. Surely your family will be in need of some funds. This is where my people can be of good help to you. Come, let us talk to one another about this challenge. Let me help you my friend."

"No thanks Torrez. I can figure this out on my own."

"Oh you can, can you? Well, I will be interested to see how you manage that my friend. Who will hire a young Latino like you? There are no baseball teams hiring batboys, I fear. But maybe you will find something for a scholar-athlete like yourself. Good luck with that. And when you have given up, come find me. I can always be found. While you are doing your homework, I am holding court in the back room of Sal's Pool Hall. You know it, just around the corner. They have the best shaved ice in town. Remember, I am always here for you."

Alberto waved him off and headed on into the locker room. But as the weeks passed and father lingered first in hospital, then in the easy chair at home, Alberto found no one who would employ him. He began to think about Torrez and his offer. What could it hurt? Torrez would probably give him the easy stuff at first. He could earn some quick money—maybe just for six months or so, maybe a year, and then Papa would be back at work and he could get out of the gang.

So that's how he found himself heading to Sal's Pool Hall one Saturday afternoon. Was it only by chance that Father Thomas met him a block from the building?

"Alberto, just the man I was looking for. I have some things to talk to you about. Won't you join me on a walk to the parish."

"But Father, I have bus…"

"Yes I am sure you have business to take care of, but it can wait. Come along now with me."

Reluctantly, Alberto obliged.

When they got to the Parish, Father Thomas ushered him into his office. "Sit down, sit down please, I will make us a cup of tea."

Alberto obediently sat, restlessly shaking his knee as Father poured the tea, adding two lumps of sugar and handed it to him before settling himself behind his desk.

"Alberto your family has been very much on my mind these days. Your father is healing slowly, and this is a terrible burden for you all, but most especially for you. It is so hard for a young Latino to find work in this town. Much less work capable of replacing a grown man's income. And you with your good marks in school and your success on the baseball field—you must be feeling quite a bit of pressure. Tell me, where were you heading just now?"

"Father, I, I—you must understand why…"

"Never mind young man, this is not the confessional. I'll ask no more about your whereabouts. Because I have a solution. I have been to your father's employer. He feels very bad about what has happened. Your papa is among his most valued employees, and he is feeling the pinch of his loss. He has agreed to hire you after school. There is plenty to do at the landscaping business. It is good work—honest work. And he will pay you the same as the grown men. It won't totally make up for your father's income, but soon he will be back at work, and between the two of you, you can make ends meet."

"But Father, what of my baseball?"

"I am afraid you will have to give it up my boy. It is too bad about that. But it is better than playing baseball on the prison yard team. Which is where you would end up if you had made your way into Sal's today."

It wasn't easy. Alberto missed his baseball mightily. But the work was outdoors, and it was physical, and used up a great deal of his restless energy. He grew strong muscles, and it was good to be working the land again. It brought back memories of Guatemala.

One bright clear afternoon, while working out northwest of the city, he even saw on the horizon the faint outline of mountains. His heart lifted just a tad.

The foreman noticed him too. On breaks he asked

him about his studies and helped him with his English. He saw to it that Alberto graduated on time, and he helped him through the citizenship process.

On the 4th of July, the summer of his graduation, Alberto and his family rose before dawn to travel to Charlottesville. Their car climbed the mountain (quite beautiful mountain at that) up to Monticello, where Alberto received his citizenship. The gathered crowd cheered. Alberto's heart sang.

Now that he was a naturalized citizen, the landscaping business owner could hire him on as a foreman too. Eventually, he agreed to bring him on as a partner in the business. Alberto was doing far better than he had ever dreamed in high school.

But sometimes his heart still called out for his grandmother, and the little village he remembered so fondly. He longed to return, if only for a visit. Though the town was much safer now, Grandmama was struggling. A letter had arrived.

Dearest Family,

 I fear I am not doing well. It seems that the smoke from the wood stove all these years has made my lungs weak. I will not be able to visit you again. I am too weak to travel. Though I miss you terribly, I remind you and myself—we are still under the same big sky.

   Much love,
   Abuela

"That's the last straw," Alberto thought. He just couldn't take it any more. He had to see his grandmother, He could take her an air conditioner. The little village now had electricity, and Grandmama could use it to make her lungs better. Alberto applied for a passport, and made arrangements to use his vacation time for the visit. He found a portable air conditioning unit, and had it shipped to his grandmother's village. ("I will install it when I get there," he thought.) He saved for the airfare and finally was able to book his ticket. The time came for him to leave.

The afternoon before the trip, with his passport, plane ticket and a hefty wallet of cash in his pocket, Alberto walked into the convenience store to buy a nice fountain coke and some snacks for the trip. Just as he was putting his cash down on the counter a masked man walked into the store brandishing a gun.

"Hands up in the air everyone." Alberto felt the cold barrel of a gun against his temple. "Give me every dime in that cash drawer or this guy is toast."

There was something familiar in the gunman's voice. "Torrez...Torrez, is that you? It is, isn't it? It's me, Alberto from high school, you remember."

"Ah, Alberto, the one whose father was injured. The one I offered to help. Yes, yes I remember. Now shut up. I meant what I said. I'll kill you no matter who you are if that guy doesn't give me the money."

"Torrez, you can't do this. They will kill *you* if you do. They won't allow a Latina who has killed an American citizen to live—and only over the change in a cash drawer? Are you crazy? Is your life, and mine, worth so little? Please, I beg you. Don't ruin your life and mine too. Put the gun down."

"You, an American citizen? Hah! That can't be. It is too hard. How can it be?"

"Years ago Torrez, I almost did join your gang. I was on my way to Sal's when Father Thomas stopped me. He found me a job--a good job. I worked hard, and I studied and many people helped me. Now I am a citizen. Tomorrow I leave for Guatemala to see my grandmother. I have worked hard Torrez. Please don't do this to me. Or to yourself. Here, I will give you some money--$100. I will gladly give it to you. Just go and make something better of yourself. Please go."

Through his mask tears began to form in Torrez's eyes.

Alberto took the risk of reaching into his pocket. He pulled out two crisp $50 bills. "Here Torrez, take them. Take them and go. Let go of this life of sorrow. Go."

Torrez took the money and fled the store. No one followed him.

As the sun rose over the mountain Alberto arrived in the village. Before going to Grandmama's door he paused to watch the day break, to smell the aroma of beans and rice cooking, to breath in the fresh crisp summer air. He offered a word of gratitude as he took in the beauty of his childhood home.

And then he walked on to find Grandmama standing at the door waiting for him—what a wonderful sight to behold. They embraced and Alberto said, "Now, my sweet Grandmama we *are truly* under the same big sky."

CHAPTER 8 WHEN GIRLS GROW

GLENDA KOTCHISH and JANE WILSON

Irish Twins

by Jane Ellen Holliday Wilson

The drama of *their* birthdays overshadows any memory of my own special day. In fact, I can only grasp one precious birthday memory--my fifth birthday--my entire nursery school class was there! (It was a shining moment in my social career, never to be eclipsed. But that is not the story to be told here.)

This is the story of being sister to a pair of *Irish twins* -- two siblings born on the same day a year apart. Not such a PC term these days, but back then we thought nothing of it. Generally speaking, my birthday was an "oh by the way," a bit part in the gentle theater of our family life when compared to *the big day*--October 15--the day that *both* of my sisters were born! Exactly one year apart!

It made for fantastic dinner conversation, "Did you know that my sister and I are *Irish twins*, born on the same day, a year apart?"

"No, how amazing! How did you manage the celebration?"

"Well, we did it together every year. I never had a cake of my own until I went away to college," Sarah would quip, her self-sacrifice softened with just the hint of a smile at the corners of her lips. I think she rather enjoyed the whole thing.

"I don't think she ever forgave me for being born on her first birthday." Catherine would add, and the conversation would go on from there.

Note that no one ever turned to me (the only other

101

child in the family) and said, "And tell us about your birthday, Alison." What could possibly be interesting about that?

I don't think Momma ever really came to terms with the whole thing. Bless her heart; she made a valiant effort around the affair. But all her labors only served to put an exclamation point on the challenge at hand.

The celebration was, in fact, the hardest part. What on earth was she supposed to do? How could she make one celebrant feel special without ignoring the other? How could anyone really keep the comparisons at bay?

To tell the truth, I don't think she ever got over it all. There's a picture of Sarah "blowing out" her one candle on her first birthday cake. (Sarah did actually have this one birthday cake all to herself.) And the story is that Momma immediately left for the hospital after the picture was snapped. Pictures of my mother took on a hint of exhaustion after that day.

My arrival nearly blew the top off her head on the birthday subject. Now what? Poor Momma; so determined to divide the pie into equal parts. What was she to do with me--the child that was forced to spend the day watching the other family siblings get spoiled?

To Momma it was sort of like Christmas but you skipped one of your babies and had to watch her sit there while the others opened all the loot. Or at least this was the way she saw it. Mothers can have the softest, most uncontrollably tender hearts at times.

Momma finally decided to solve this inconvenient piece of the problem by getting a little something for me to unwrap too. In this department unfortunately, her Scotch ancestry often kicked in. She just couldn't resist the opportunity to get me something *I needed* and pretend it was a present--those humiliating Kelly green, double elastic pants for example. I was a profound tomboy at the time (still am for that matter) and the boys in the neighborhood teased me no end for showing up in those silly things to play kickball. Never mind that I had the best toe in the business--could kick that ball into the next yard every time. Maybe that's why, to this day, I hate to wear pants. But I digress.

I never told her that I didn't care about a present, that I was really needed on the kickball field, and did I have to hang around to watch my prissy ol' sisters open their matching electric curler sets?

Actually, it wasn't that bad. All the comparisons, and compromises, shared cake, shared parties and shared dinner menus did provide some pretty keen fireworks from time to time. And to tell the truth--I, the generally picked on, but for once ignored kid sister--I rather enjoyed the show.

GLENDA KOTCHISH and JANE WILSON

A Birthday

by Glenda Mace Kotchish

The kitchen table,
Daddy, eating his breakfast--a work day, a school day.
Mama at the stove.
A card on the table for me.

A girly-girl card
Pink, lace and frills
for a 1960's child
Five dollars inside.
Such a surprise.

I've always thought it was Daddy--
His five-dollar gift--
Him the one remembering my 15th birthday.
It was a lot of money back then.
It was a big deal to me.

It's only now that I realize
It was probably my mother--
who selected and purchased
the card--
my mostly unloving mother.

She's gone now--my mother. It took a long time--85 years--actually just ten days short of her 86th birthday. I'll tell you right now, it was sad, a sad life--hers and mine and the whole family.

Poor Daddy--he took care of her from the time she was nineteen until he died and then after he died--well his social security took care of her.

My sister and I tried to help her but she'd turn on us. It was like trying to cuddle a tiger. Sometimes you thought you had a kitten in your lap but then it would transform into a wild thing and strike out at you. We walked away many times--bleeding--angry and sad at the same time. Then we'd come back and try to nurture her and it would all repeat--time and time again.

She had a smile that could make you angry. It was sarcastic--like she knew something you didn't. For instance, the time my sister found her a great place to live and it took a lot of work to arrange everything. My mother was going off about my sister and how bad she was at the time. Mama had a habit of saying "that Susan," or "that Roy," and you knew *that* person was about to be crucified. On this occasion when my sister was the *that*, I told my mother that Susan was the one who loved her the most, and worked hard to find her a nice place to live. My mother looked at me with that awful smile of hers. I knew what she was thinking. It was *the Lord* that did it--not my sister. My mother had a way of taking anything good you did and giving the credit to *the Lord*, making you nothing.

As she lay on her deathbed, the day before she actually died, I went to see her. She was skin and bones--hardly breathing. It was hard. It was always hard to go see her. You never knew what you'd get. You had to keep your guard up. Sometimes she'd want to hug and kiss, and other times she'd look at you with her dark brown eyes and scare the hell out of you. She was a Christian. But she could have just as easily been a witch--the way she could look at you. On this day there was little to be said, really. I heard myself say as much and I told her I was sorry that her life was so hard.

So maybe you get the picture. Maybe you don't. I

could tell you some stories. Don't get me wrong. There was some happiness too. She shopped for Christmas and made us birthday cakes and if we were sick, she'd tend us. But for the most part--in the end--it was just sad--all round.

I never gave her much credit for anything. I just didn't trust her. And I reckon that's why I have had a hard time trusting anyone to this day. I'm learning though.

Thinking back now, I guess she *was* the one who remembered my birthday and bought the card. I have to give her that--don't you think? She was my mother after-all.

GLENDA KOTCHISH and JANE WILSON

A WINTER'S DREAM

by Glenda Mace Kotchish

It was January 19, 1961 and the snow started falling. It continued all day and throughout the following day. We'd never seen anything like it in our southern town--fourteen inches of snow. It paralyzed the city. In our climate, we usually get *a dusting,* a tease of snow. Sometimes we'd get two or three inches, just enough to have a short sleigh ride in the park. But this particular snow was monumental. Nothing was moving, not the buses, not the trains and certainly not the cars--even with snow chains on the tires. Then two weeks later another snow--seventeen inches fell from the skies this time.

Schools were closed for a month.

We made snow cream with snow, sugar and vanilla. At night after work, Daddy took us to the park with our sleigh. The city had put 50 gallon barrels out, filled them with wood and lit them for light and warmth. We'd warm our hands by the barrels after each trip down the hill. For us, there were the gentle slopes of the park for us. The older kids ventured to the steeper hills and the frozen stream that ran through the park. It was a happy time.

Right after the first snow, my sister invited a girl friend to our house for a sleepover. It was the first time she'd ever had a sleepover. They were teenagers--just barely, but old enough to feel their superiority in age so they ignored me--the kid.

My sister and I shared a bedroom, upstairs. My father had finished off one room in the attic for us when our baby brother was born. It was a nice room with dormer windows and plenty of space and light. He installed a vent in the floor, directly over the downstairs floor furnace--to heat the room. It was clever. Not only did heat rise but (known only to my sister and me) you could hear what was going on downstairs by listening at the vent--not that much ever went on.

For the sleepover I was to sleep downstairs for the night, in my baby brother's room. But as it happened, that evening my mother and father had an argument and my mother was so *miffed* that she decided to sleep in my brother's room. She sent me to sleep with my father. When I went into their room, Daddy was already under the covers--snoring a little. He was a thin man and there was plenty of room in the bed for me. But I felt odd, actually too old to be sleeping with my father but too young to join in with my sister and her friend. I too was *miffed*, so I laid down on the bed on top of the covers and went to sleep.

Was it the chill of the night that made me dream? Or was it the vague feeling of discomfort of sleeping with my father? Perhaps both. Regardless, I remember that dream to this day.

It is winter. A deep snow is on the ground. I am in our front yard. Two teenage boys, with long hair, slicked back on their heads, shiny with hair-cream are coming down the street. They are wearing black leather jackets. They are skating on ice skates--very fast, toward me. As they approach I realize they mean to do me harm. I am terrified but I cannot run.

Suddenly, as can happen only in a dream--it is summer and I am in the front yard of our house once again. I am so relieved that the snow is gone, the boys are gone and they cannot harm me because without snow and ice, their skates are useless. Then in the distance I see the two teenagers approaching. To my horror they are wearing their skates. The summer heat and lack of snow does not deter them from tearing down the street. The skate blades make sparks on the pavement as they race closer and closer to me. There is no escape from them, winter or summer.

I awoke, cold and shaking. I slipped under the covers on my side of the bed shivering in the dark, unable to fall back to sleep.

The next day I developed a cold. I couldn't shake the dream from my consciousness. I was afraid of the snow, the frozen roads, the ease of travel it provided would-be skaters, even though there was no one I knew who owned skates or would know how to use them if they did. In fact, I didn't know any teenage boys, at all--in my family, in the neighborhood or at my school. The few boys at church were unlike the boys in my dream. They were well groomed and polite.

But I was terrified. We went to church. I imagined the skaters hiding behind the curtains of the baptismal pool. I stuck close to my sister. I avoided being alone in rooms. I was afraid to go to sleep. Fear consumed me.

Then the second snow storm hit. I did not go sleigh riding in the park. I did not gather snow for snow cream. I stayed in the house waiting for the snow to melt.

Finally, the schools reopened. Snow was still on the ground but the roads were clear and even the small side streets were passable. Since my sister went to junior-high, she rode the bus; but my elementary school was only five blocks from our house so I walked to school each day. I had made the trip since kindergarten, at first with my sister, then (for the past two years)--alone. Now, I was afraid as I gather my books and my lunch and walked out to the end of the sidewalk.

I glanced down the street and I froze. I saw two teenage boys walking toward me. They were walking in the middle of the street. They were talking to each other. When they were a few yards away, I half turned to run back in our house. But I was paralyzed as they continued to walk toward me. They passed without even a glance my way.

My adrenalin dropped and I breathed out. I walked to the gate, opened it and make my way to school.

* *For months as a child, the dream haunted me. It was only many, many years later--as a grown woman, reading about Carl Jung, that I came to understand how the unconscious of my eleven-year-old mind was preparing me for growing up.*

CHAPTER 9 GETTING THERE

GLENDA KOTCHISH and JANE WILSON

It's Time to Make the Cookies

Jane Ellen Holliday Wilson

The cookies—playfulness. If I stop to make the cookies I'll get totally off track—my diet—my rigor—my routine. I might have some fun. But who has time for that—or who even *dares* with all this mourning hanging over us?

The cookies take so long. And when the job is done, there are *so* many to deal with. And then I would have to share them with somebody and who is there for that? Where will they go? Maybe *he* could take them to the office to share with all the droopy faces there. He could show them that there is life after all this gloom. The relentless gloom of losing their leader. So suddenly. So senselessly.

He might sneak one along the way. Should I let him? Do I really have a choice—poor grieving thing—how dare I deny him? Twenty-five years of working side-by-side, lunching together, all snatched away in the blink of an eye.

Might these sweet little nibbles cheer us up along the way?

If I make them, I will surely lose my discipline. I will eat them all. And, if I don't, he will. And he won't stop— how dare he! He will lose himself, and I will lose myself, and we will dissolve into chaos after all these pounds we have worked so hard to lose, find their way back onto our abdomens!

Yes, I will have to send some to the office.

I wonder, if I would feel lonely without a daughter helping me make them—those sweet girls who are now off on their own, living their lives—one, or the other, or both

115

or all of them (my step-darlings love to make them too). They always cut out the heart shapes, and apply the pink frosting. Would it be any fun at all to undertake this by myself?

Well, I could send them to Nattie in Philly for a Valentine treat, and Kaitlin and Elias and Jack in D.C., and Abbey in Durham. (Can't send them to Lindsay in the middle of the ocean on her sailing boat. That makes me sad.) But I can invite Gretchen over for a few.

So what if they all got them late, wouldn't my magical cookies still cheer them? They might even squeal with delight!

And…I might have fun. I might have to stop being a police person—the strict and structured one. Keeping the traffic moving along by the rules. Yuck!

I think I'll make the cookies.

Finally! She Came Back to Herself

by Jane Ellen Holliday Wilson

It had been a long slog—an ugly, endless, physically demanding, intellectually devoid slog to the finish.

At one point her husband had sheepishly volunteered, "Helen honey, it might help if you would just remember how to smile."

Gentle Harvey may as well have struck her with a bolt of lightning. Helen, the person who *always* smiled—famous for her smile in some circles—had to be reminded to do so!

The loving reprimand called her to her senses—not entirely—but at least it made her aware that she had lost something of herself in the last months. Something that Harvey, and her elderly parents, and her children counted on.

Years ago—during the dark years—Helen had relied on that smile to keep everyone from knowing that her world was crumbling from the inside out; that her now ex-husband was slipping away. Her smile was used to reassure the children, to keep her neighbors' and relatives' questions at bay; and even to fool her priest into believing that hers was the perfect family.

As she trudged through the divorce, the single parenting, the finding of a new career, the dreadful blind dates, the teenage years (oh my God, the teenage years!), the smile never wavered.

So how was it that now, now that sweet Harvey was securely in her life, loving her every day; that her children were through their gauntlets and well launched; her plans laid—the challenging tasks of downsizing, sorting, packing almost complete—how was it that Harvey, her precious Harvey had to say, "smile please"?

She paused.

She thought.

She closed her eyes.

She reminded herself to inhale deeply, and it came to her.

Finally, after all these years, all this struggle—it was safe not to smile.

And in that moment, she came back to herself – and for the first time in a very long time—Helen *honestly* smiled.

SOLD

by Glenda Mace Kotchish

Sold!
It was music to her ears.
So what if the market hadn't fully recovered,
She'd take it.
That's a big yes. It's yours baby, all yours.
Sign right here on the dotted line.
She'd take the money and run--thank you very much--nice
doing business with you.

Out the door. Let it slam behind her.
She skipped down the sidewalk, waving the cashier's check
and humming a little tune: La de da,
Look at me!

No more running ads "house for rent".
No more craigslist postings,
No more competition with foreclosures, short-sales, and
an abundance of rental properties,

No more peculiar people calling,
No more applications, application fees, credit reports,
credit report fees,
No more meeting strange people.

No more, "Please make an exception and rent to me and my family."
No more looking for the non-existent *nice family*,
No more, "Let me tell you my sob story."
No more falling for your *sob story*.

No more changing locks, buying keys,
No more leases,
No more being last on someone's priority list to get paid,
No more, "But it's Christmas, no rent money for you 'til next year."

No more, "Call the plumber, my kid flushed a doll down the toilet."
No more stacking firewood on the wooden porch,
No more $1000 in termite treatments,
No more ants, mice and exterminators.

No more, "I love you," one day and, "I'll sue you," the next,
No more, "Just how many people are living in my house?"
No more, "I just have one cat" (that multiplies).

No more scathing emails,
No more psychotic phone calls,
No more returned checks, non-sufficient funds and corresponding fees,
No more collecting rent and, *Voice mailbox is full* messages.

No more *Pay or Quit* letters,
No more evictions,
No more sheriff with his drawn gun and his, "All clear"

announcement,
No more moving stuff to the curb.

No more painting over shiny, school bus yellow walls,
No more black rooms, pink rooms, princess chandeliers,
stars on the ceiling,
No more holes in the walls,
No more broken appliances.

No more filthy bathrooms (is that a dead mouse in the
drawer? No just a hair extension--thank the Lord.),
No more stripping out cables,
No more patching the holes from cables, wires and
assorted hardware.

No more trips to the dump with abandoned shower
curtains, drapes, shades, lamps, mattresses, bed rails,
broken furniture, moldy pillows, dishes, stacks of wood.
No more mopping, cleaning, dusting, painting, scrubbing
up after other people,
No more…
No more anything...ever again.
Praise the Lord.
Hallelujah.
She's in heaven…

GLENDA KOTCHISH and JANE WILSON

CHAPTER 10 FOR THE BIRDS

GLENDA KOTCHISH and JANE WILSON

In the Garden

A Summer Solstice Story

Jane Ellen Holliday Wilson

The longest day of the year is over and now we head
Inch by inch
day by day

Into the darkness

There is a sadness in
The garden today

It happened while we were
Away

On a little outing
To ease our own
Recent sadnesses--

A father lost
Another forgetting
A daughter suffering
A pair of mothers
Wobbling

But the garden sadness--
I fear--
May be of the worst
Variety

Mother Robin's baby has
Drowned

They are clearly an extraordinary couple
Those two--Momma and Papa Robin

They built a large nest right in the
Thickest part of the mock cherry tree

That first morning we were here
Groggy from unpacking
Standing at the kitchen window
I noticed something glittering
In that old tree

As I opened the door, out popped Papa Robin
Pretty as you please

He landed on the fence post and began to sing
The most uproarious of songs

Pride mixed with admonition--"Come out here and see me
But don't you get to close now."

I drew closer to the edge of the porch and noticed that,
attached to that glittery thing
Was a plump and spacious nest

Turns out the shiny thing was a carefully attached *nosegay*
of Christmas tinsel
Silver, red, gold

As I watched the couple, I learned how very pleased they
were with their
Unconventional home

And to me it seemed a happy miniature of our own
Grey porch
Flashy red door
And so on.
I thought we had chosen well indeed

As my husband and I settled in
Began to dig in the dirt
Set up our feeders
Saucy Robin seemed
To delight in his good
Fortune--as did we

New soil, juicy worms
Why--even a bird bath below the nest
No need for foraging afar anymore

The couple didn't bat an eye at the invasion of
Sparrows, finches, grackles and so forth--all showing
Up for our top-of-the-line birdseed

Those two were tough--
They could withstand anything

But it must have been the storm that rolled through
On the night we were away that did it,

Because there she was this morning--
Sweet little fledgling thing--
Floating in the birdbath

Would she have survived the fall if she had landed on the
Hard pebbles instead? Should we move the bath?
Change things up?
Those are questions for later

Now, what is important is that I handle this sweet child
with some dignity--
The way I would want for my own--
For her mother's and her father's sake

I get the shovel
I dig a hole in the hard, dry ground
Right under that tree

I try to make it as deep as I can
I place the sweet child inside
Cover her up
Place two sticks in the form of a cross on the breast of her
grave
And another straight up at her head

I go into the house
Gather some flowers--
The ones left over from my own sweet daughter's

Housewarming bouquet

I come back to place the flowers over her
Only to find
Another stick has been stuck in the ground beside her

Hmmm…..

I smile, look around to find what I already know to be
true--
There are no other humans in this garden
There are only sad robins.

I place my flowers on her grave and offer up a hope--
A prayer
As each day shortens, so too may the sadness of
Momma and Papa robin.

GLENDA KOTCHISH and JANE WILSON

Pretty Boy

Glenda Mace Kotchish

My sister, Linda saw him first. All bright and proud of himself--whistling away, calling out to her "pretty girl," followed by a drawn-out wolf call. Linda called to me, "Come quick!"

I got there in a flash, and there he was!

"Oh, he's so pretty," I said--because there he was-- perched in our umbrella tree on a low branch, blue feathers with yellow accents and a little yellow beak tweeting, "pretty girl, pretty girl."

We both laughed.

"I've never seen a talking bird," I said.

"Me neither," said my sister, as she stepped closer to the branch and stood on tiptoes. She stretched to her full ten-year old height. She slowly reached out her hand and offered her index finger to the little bird.

To our amazement, he hopped on. I jumped, but Linda held steady and looked over the top of his head at me, smiling broadly. "His feet feel funny," she said, "very soft, though."

She stood still and whispered, "Go get Mama."

"But he'll fly away while I'm gone," I protested.

"No, he won't," she assured me. "He's not a wild bird. He's a pet bird. Run quick."

So I ran into the house and found my mother. "Come quick. Linda has a bird."

"A bird?"

"Yes, a bird--a blue bird."

"Is he dead?" she asked.

"No, no Ma'am, he's on her finger and he's talking to her."

"Talking to her?"

131

"Yes, come quick before he flies away."

I grabbed her hand and pulled her out the door and into the yard. Linda was seated now under the umbrella tree. The little bird was still perched on her finger. He was wiggling and chirping, "Pretty girl, pretty girl."

Linda looked up as we approached. "Mama, look--a little bird, and it's tame. It's not scared at all. He keeps calling me *pretty girl.*" She looked at my mother pleadingly, "Can we keep him?"

"Well," my mother frowned and drew out the word.

At this the bird turned his head from side to side and eyed my mother. He let out two long wolf-call whistles and chirped, "Pretty girl, pretty girl."

My mother *was* gorgeous. She had brown hair cut in a stylish pageboy, deep brown eyes, arched brows, perfect red lips and a curvy figure. Even the boys in my kindergarten ogled her when she dropped me off at school. I had no idea she was so pretty until they told me, "Your mama is p-r-e-t-t-y", admiringly. Until then she was just my mama, but on that day she became my pretty mama. So it was not surprising to me that this bird called her "pretty girl" when he saw her.

My mother said "Oh my!" raising a hand to her mouth. She thought for a moment then said, "Well, we will have to think about it." Hedging, she added, "We'll ask your Daddy when he gets home."

Soon the neighborhood kids and other mothers had gathered round in our yard looking at the talking bird. And still he stayed, right there, on Linda's finger.

"It's a parakeet," someone said.

"It must be someone's pet that has flown away," remarked Mrs. Brandie, the neighbor from next-door. "We had a bird once and I think we still have the cage." She sent her son to fetch it from her attic.

We cleaned the cage, dried it out and presented it to the bird who happily hopped into it and sat on the little swing. He started singing "Pretty Boy, Pretty Boy." That's how we came to learn his name. He was a wise bird and must have known who he had to persuade, because all afternoon he looked at my mother and sang out "Pretty girl, pretty girl", finally winning her over.

We gave him water and Daddy was called and told to stop by the store on his way home and buy birdseed. Pretty Boy became a member of our household.

My sister and I learned to line his cage with newspaper and change it. We bought him toys, bells and let him fly around the house.

Pretty Boy was entirely a lady's bird. He kissed us and wiggled his little feathers and sang out, "Pretty girl," to not only my mother, my sister and me but to any girl who walked down the street. This was embarrassing to my father.

"People will think it's me shouting out to women, when it's only that darn bird! Somebody shut the door so he can't see outside."

Pretty Boy did not fancy men at all. He especially disliked my father. At every opportunity, Pretty Boy would land on Daddy's head and peck it. One morning he swooped down to the breakfast table and landed on my father's cereal bowl and began eating the toasted wheat. Daddy swatted Pretty Boy away with some curses and not a little force. Pretty Boy landed in the kitchen sink dish water. He hopped out, unruffled his feathers and squawked loudly at my father. I'm fairly certain that Pretty Boy thought of Daddy as his arch rival.

But we loved that bird. He amused our friends as much as he did us. On nice days we would take his cage outside and let him have fresh air. When my father wasn't home, he had the run of the house.

When he first came to us, my sister and I worried that his former owner would discover we had Pretty Boy and come to our door one day and take him away. We imagined a family, like ours riding around in their car looking for the little bird, calling "Pretty Boy, Pretty Boy, where are you?" But after a few weeks we relaxed and Pretty Boy became our bird.

Pretty Boy got Christmas presents and special treats for all the holidays. We were rewarded with his calls of "Pretty girl, pretty girl"--a boost to our self-esteem. And to my father's chagrin, whenever Pretty Boy spied my mother, he'd let out one of his wolf-calls.

Two years passed happily until one early spring day when my sister decided to take Pretty Boy's cage outside and let him have some fresh air. It was a breezy day and no sooner had she set the cage down on the picnic table than a wind came by and blew it over. The little cage door fell open and Pretty Boy flew out and up into the tree. Then he spread his wings and was gone.

We were devastated. My sister was in tears. "It's all my fault, it's all my fault," she moaned.

We had no time for laying blame. The two of us ran down the street looking in all the trees, calling "Pretty Boy, Pretty Boy." When my father came home from work, he found us crying "How could he leave us and just fly away like that?" we sobbed. Daddy took us in the car, to look for Pretty Boy further a field--probably all the while, secretly hoping we would not find the bird.

Now it was our turn to hang out the car windows, looking up into the trees and to call "Pretty Boy, Pretty Boy where are you?"

We looked until it got dark. We didn't find Pretty Boy. We hoped he found another home with some other pretty girls to live with. We hoped he was safe and happy and not scared out there all alone. It was hard not knowing.

We never got another bird because who could *ever* replace Pretty Boy?

My sister and I sometimes reminisce. One of us will ask the other, "Do you remember Pretty Boy?"

Oh, yes" the other will respond and we both smile broadly thinking of the little bird who thought we were his "Pretty girls."

The Things He's Done

by Jane Ellen Holliday Wilson

Teach me the language of birds
Teach me the habits of birds
Teach me the feeding of birds
Teach me the housing of birds
Teach me the comfort of birds

Teach me this:
When all else has left you
          Enjoy the birds
            And all will be well

~~~

When I was 16, I had to ask one of my best guy friend to the prom because no one asked me, and in those days this was considered total and complete *girl shame*. It was, to say the least, a tad demoralizing; especially when you consider that *I* was the chair of the prom decorating committee. Even though this friend *was* a good guy, it just wasn't the same as having a *real* date. You know, every girl's dream--or at least every 1973, small town girl's dream. I know, I know, most of America was already well into to the feminist revolution by then, but not our town, and certainly not my household.

The big day came and I was trying with all my 16-year-old spirit to keep my chin up, and the tears in check behind my green eyes, as we put the finishing touches on the high school gym. *Stairway to Heaven* or some such slightly edgy popular tune was the theme around which we built our props.

I came home just in time to shower, throw electric curlers in my hair and get into my home-made ruffly yellow gown for the big night. I thought I had done a pretty good job thus far of disguising my feelings. After all, I was a brave girl in those days--practiced at giving as little away as possible.

So, when Daddy called me outside I was perturbed to say the least, "Daddy, it's prom night. Can't you see I am trying to get ready on time? I can't come out there in the yard right now!"

"I know what night it is, Darlin'. Just throw on a robe and come on out anyway. It'll only take a minute. There's something you need to see," came the answer in his deep base voice. He was, after all, a formidable 6'5" kind of guy. (This could be one of the reasons the boys didn't ask me out--fear of my father.) I knew better than to argue.

So he got me out the screen door.

"Come on out here. Come on now."

"Daddy, what on earth is it. I haven't got time!"

"Come on, just come on out here." He motioned to a specific spot in the backyard, "Right here."

"OK," those hard electric curlers still bound to my scalp with those uncomfortable wire pins. They were enough to make anyone cranky all on their own. "Here I am. Now what?"

"Lie down on the ground."

I looked him in the eye, "Are you crazy? Can't you see I have these curlers in my just washed hair?"

"It's not going to ruin anything. Just come on, lie down here with me. Hurry or you'll miss it." In agony, tense with misery and stress, I obeyed.

I laid down.

Daddy lay down beside me.

He pointed up to the sky, "Now just relax, and look up there."

"Where, Daddy?"

"Right there, Sweetie. There she is. See her?"

My eye caught sight of her--that majestic creature. Her wings spread wide, she looked to be just circling around and around.

"She's a hawk," he continued as I gazed up. "Watch her. She's just riding the current. See Honey, she knows that it's a beautiful day--nice breeze, pretty clouds," he gently took my hand. "And she better not miss the opportunity to enjoy it, because beautiful days don't come along every day.

"You can go to a silly old prom any day sweetheart, with anybody, but beautiful days are meant to be enjoyed no matter what. The hawk knows that. She's not worried about her hair or her clothes. She knows she is just right."

And then he turned his eyes away from the sky and toward me, "And you are too...just right."

With that, he kissed my tear stained cheek and sent me back into the house to finish my primping--a little less deflated, a tad more grateful, and slightly more aware that this *was* a beautiful day.

GLENDA KOTCHISH and JANE WILSON

.

Birds

by Glenda Mace Kotchish

My mother liked birds.

When I was a child, a parakeet showed up on our doorstep one summer and stayed for two years before flying the coup. His name was Pretty Boy. We knew this because he told us. He loved women, especially my mother. He'd see her and whistle out a wolf call and say "Pretty girl."

After he left us, for many years there were no other birds.

Then my youngest sister decided to raise cockatoos. Prissy somehow got the male and female to mate--leaving them in the same cage probably did it. I think I remember Prissy telling me that the male would peck all the feathers from the female's head--or maybe it was the other way around. Did the birds use the plucked feathers for a nest? I can't recall but when those little eggs hatched my sister had to feed the tiny birds with an eyedropper every 15 minutes. So when someone says "you eat like a bird," don't be deceived--those little suckers can put it away.

Prissy was pretty successful at raising birds. Before we knew it she had a house full of chirpers. None of them actually talked--English or any other language except their own. And Prissy spent a great deal of time changing newspaper in the bottom of cages, and a great deal of money on birdseed, toys and paraphernalia. I think she had it in her mind to have a bird business and sell the little buggers. She actually did sell a couple.

One Christmas when she was in the throes of bird breeding, the entire family was invited over for a

Christmas get-together. Her house pretty much resembled a bat cave at that point except for the lighted Christmas tree. It was pretty dark. We all sat around and ate Christmas snacks and watched TV. My mother, who--as I said--was fond of birds, got one of the cockatoos out of its cage and let it walk around on her finger and hand. My mother was very fastidious and when the bird pooped on her chest--right on her Christmas sweater--I was surprised that she didn't make a fuss about it. She got a tissue out of her pocket and mopped it up and continued to tweet, tweet at the bird. That was it for me--the snacking was over. I have a weak stomach.

Eventually Prissy gave up the bird-raising farm. I don't know what she did with the birds--either gave them away, or sold them. So the family was bird-less for a while.

A few years later, someone gave my mother a cockatoo--cage and all. This one *could* talk. And it learned new words all the time. I forget its name. The manager of the apartment building where my mother lived gave it to her. The bird was driving her (the manager) crazy. It seems it would make a siren (ambulance-like) scream when it wanted attention--sounded exactly like an ambulance and just as loud.

I think the bird was a male. So from here on out I'll call it "he." Anyway, "he" kept my mother company. She taught it bible scriptures. He learned her name--"Josey."

All went well, actually as well as could be expected given my mother's tendency to stir up the worst in people and they reacted in kind. As I was saying, all went well until one day my mother accidentally left a pot cooking on the stove and it caught fire.

She had the presence of mind to put out the fire and air out the apartment. But she was immediately put on the chopping block at the apartment complex. Did I mention the apartment complex was for senior citizens? It was also affiliated with a Christian organization. It even had "Christian" as part of its name. My mother loved the idea that she was living amongst other Christians. However, the fact that the residents didn't always act very Christ-like was a constant source of distress among the general population--especially my mother, who of course could be "at fault" herself pretty often. But I blame the whole situation on the management. They should have implemented some kind of screening process to separate the wheat from the chaff, as it were. Then, on the other hand--the occupancy rate would be darn near close to zero--I guess. Who's to judge?

Anyway, on the day in question--the fire--well more smoke than actual fire--the manager insisted that my mother vacate her apartment. I was called in--first by my mother and then by the apartment management. Then before I arrived on the scene--the police were called. Oh yes, things escalated pretty fast around there. The manager and Mom got into a shouting match. Then the manager pulled out all the stops and insisted that my mother was demented, could cause "harm to herself and to others."

While this was being debated, the other residents had circled the wagons and were taking potshots at my mother from the sidelines. I tried to defuse the situation by asking the onlookers/ hecklers to go back to their homes and leave it to us. This provoked the manager who informed me that I wasn't in charge and, "These people have every right to be here." The police were being pretty silent and standoffish. The manager, at this point insisted that the police either make me and my mother leave the premises, or arrest us both for trespassing. In the end, my mother went home with me for a few days while we sorted out everything. Neither of us were jailed--although at the time I did call my husband to tell him to come over immediately and to bring a lawyer with him. The bird, however, stayed at the apartment. My mother arranged for a friend from her church to come and feed him while she was away.

Finally my mother was allowed to return to her home. The apartment had no real damage after all--not even smoke damage. But the bird had suffered major trauma from the experience. He would sit on his perch and repeat over and over, "Josey, gone. Josey, gone." It was heartbreaking--really.

To make matters worse, whenever my mother left the room, he would go into his "siren" mode. This, as you might have guessed, "gave cause" to the apartment manager to order that either the bird disappear or both the bird and my mother with him would have to go. My mother gave the bird to her church friend who had grown fond of the poor thing while tending to him. And that was pretty much the end of my mother's, as well as my "bird experiences," well that is, until today. My grandson came to visit. He has given me a bird, complete with cage to "keep me company." I'm just hoping the bird is the silent type and doesn't repeat anything I say--'cause I can pretty much guarantee it won't be Bible scriptures.

CHAPTER 11 A TRIP TO THE DESERT

GLENDA KOTCHISH and JANE WILSON

CAMEL COMPANIONSHIP

Jane Ellen Holliday Wilson

There he is—my sweet camel. He's been hiding in the back of my jewelry drawer for such a long, long time—sweet little pin, uncovered as I pack for our move to the city. I haven't visited with him for many years now. Not since I managed to find my way to the end of my trip to the desert—my long ago, extended trek through the sandy slopes. This dear little camel often adorned my lapel (rather wide in those days), a merry creature, providing a bit of cheer—a hand up--in the midst of the long, lonely journey. Offering me passage through the scorching terrain. Such a good little friend, what a comfort he was to me in those dry days.

At the time, it seemed that every moment provided a new challenge—a parched and lonely march over burning sands. Watch out for that scorpion, that snake. My *desertedness* distracted me from the beauty—the flowering, scuttling succulence that can be found even in such a place.

It was the 90's then, and I was a young mother, newly single, newly employed again, newly learning the ins and outs of computers, nonprofits, wealthy donors, disadvantaged children, parents desperate to give their children a better education. Meanwhile, I was managing carpools, making the lunches, and *making it* to school plays and birthday parties--the inevitable balancing act, a bit like sitting atop a lumpy camel, prodding through the parched and unforgiving desert.

Now the trip to that barren landscape is finished. My garden is lush; even succulent once again. My children are sturdy and strong as Joshua trees, making their own way in the world. That, at first so frightening career of mine is well established. My new life made, my new and precious love found. I have climbed successfully out of the sandy trap that, I must confess, was of my own making. (Or, did camel tie that rope around my waist and pull me out?)

As I hold him in my hand now—feel his silvery smoothness, marvel at his ageless charm, his shy grin—those days do come back to me. And now, only now, can I see the happy things--picnics at the park with my sweet things; rainbow snow cones staining their darling, delighted faces; our love for each other growing as strong as a tall cactus—roots deeply implanted.

Or the close circle of friends who gathered themselves around me, helping me manage my life. One of those good friends tapped me on the shoulder at the grocery store the other day. Wrapping me in her friendly embrace, I was instantly transported back to those days. We took a break from our shopping and sat in the café reminiscing. When she left I began to think deeply about my journey. I had to confess that I *had* become a better person as a result of that trip through the desert.

Perhaps, I will take camel out and wear him a bit, because now, I think I understand that sometimes it's only after we've left the dry patch and stepped onto fertile ground—that we are able to truly see the parting gifts the desert can bring.

A Trip to the Desert

Glenda Mace Kotchish

Adrian had never seen a desert. She'd seen pictures of course--mounds of sand, sandstorms, waves of sand, camels. And she'd seen "Alice" a sitcom TV show which was located in Phoenix, Arizona. But because there was never a scene outside of the cafe--the show could have been located anywhere--Alaska, Louisiana, New York. Nor were the actors intrinsic to Arizona. Mel, the cafe owner and cook had a New York accent. Flo, the waitress-in-residence had a southern drawl. Alice, the star, also a waitress, was from the North East--maybe Jersey. Then there was Vera--the soft spoken one--she was from nowhere in particular. And because it was reportedly *so* hot, Adrian had no desire, whatsoever, to go to Arizona.

Then one day, out of nowhere, Adrian had a change of heart--a sudden urge to go to the desert. It snuck up on her--the feeling--the idea. She herself was surprised when she spoke the words, "I have a longing to go to the desert." It was an announcement made while at an artist retreat with strangers all around her. It came out of the blue. The strangers just looked at her and nodded.

Five years passed before Adrian actually was able to go. As it was, her husband suggested the trip to the Fiesta Bowl--New Year's Day. His alma mater was to play in the bowl game. Tickets were purchased. Itineraries were planned and the whole damn family took off--across country--two thousand miles in one day from the East Coast to south west, Arizona.

The plane banked into the airport in Phoenix--earth tones, flatness--miles and miles of roads, straight lines leading to a mountain range in the west. The airliner

147

touched down and deposited the family, the two boys, Adrian and her husband in Phoenix--mission accomplished.

The sun was setting. They gather their luggage, picked up the rental car and drove to the hotel in Tempe--one of the municipalities making up the greater Phoenix area.

Adrian said to the man at the desk, "We'd like to eat dinner. What's close by? You know, a local-type restaurant?"

The man smiled and said, "You'll Love Chili's. Everyone does. And be sure to get the Presidential Margarita."

"Thanks so much," Adrian said, and they took off to find Chili's, a restaurant chain that hadn't, as yet, made it to the East Coast. It was good--the southwest food, the Presidential margarita--everything!

The next day, Adrian was the first to wake. She wanted to see the sunrise in the desert town. She slipped on shorts, a t-shirt and a jean jacket. She quietly stepped outside, leaving her sleeping family in their beds. The sun was red and golden, just coming up on the horizon. Cactus, sage bushes and palm trees were silhouetted in black with the red and gold glow of dawn behind them.

"I'm here," she whispered. "What have you for me?"

Silence. No chirping birds, buzzing bees, no car tires on the road, no crunch of gravel or breezy wind. Just the sun, the sleeping desert city and silence.

Adrian stood for a long time listening to the silence until the answer came.

"Wait and see."

She smiled. "Yes."

CHAPTER 12 SCENES FROM AN UPSTAIRS WINDOW

GLENDA KOTCHISH and JANE WILSON

THE VIEW FROM HER SECOND FLOOR BALCONY

Jane Ellen Holliday Wilson

The view from her second floor balcony was fleeting.

As hard as she was working to find a bit of rest, re-gathering, regrouping, it seemed to slip right through her hands at every turn.

People she loved kept dying, divorcing and drifting into dementia.

What was the term the doctor had used—volume stress—too many things happening at once. Well, lately that *at once* was never ending. Between children and parents and dear friends, the "late 50's" were turning out to be a long and challenging dance with the devil.

And tonight it seemed that the devil was winning.

Fifty is the new 40, all the literature said. You have life stretching out before you. Take care of yourself first. Explore your creativity, meditate, relax, practice yoga. These are the things that will help you to zip right through this exciting time of life.

Harrumph! Did anyone mention to those writers anything about the sandwich generation—the just when you could almost see some light at the end of the tunnel, the tunnel caved in gang?

But here she was now. So hard-won, this moment—4:00 in the morning—not the long, leisurely coffee drinking, sunlit hours of staring into space and writing in her journal that she was dreaming of. But it was a moment—a cloud settled in over the valley, the sun poked through, illuminating the ancient foothills, the freshness of a brand new Sunday morning seeping in. Iridescent. Refreshing.

Today there would be more grieving, more tears to mop, more caregiving, more counseling--wise words to drum up from the depths--barely learned herself before turning to offer them to others.

For now, for today, this early morning view from her second floor balcony would have to do.

Seen from Upstairs

by Glenda Mace Kotchish

In the City

From my upstairs bedroom window, I see the Crepe Myrtles. Now in bloom--white and pink, they shield me from the hot sun that scorches and peels the paint on my house in the places left unprotected by their leafy shade.

Their leaves hide the trash and glass in the street, the electric lines, cables and telephone poles as well as the mural of eyeballs, forks and pipes which is the latest craze in this historic southern city.

In the Suburbs

I raise the shade in my upstairs bedroom window. Outside the large oak spreads its sturdy branches in which the squirrels race about stopping to nibble away at new shoots, destined to line their nests.

The old man next-door sets traps for the squirrels who dare to rob his bird-feeders. He will transport his captives to unknown places further west. They sometimes find their way back home.

The old man straps on his leaf blower, points it to the ground and sends leaves into the storm drain. He makes sure that any of his neighbor's tree leaves that have landed in his space do not rest there for long. He sends them, with a gust of noisy air from his machine, back from whence they came.

The old man walks into my yard and disappears from my view. Is he on my porch?

Knock, knock, yes, he is. I hear my husband answer the door.

The old man says, "Some family members are coming over for dinner. They'll need space to park--so you'll need to move your car."

I hear, "mumble, mumble," and the sound of the door closing.

Across the street another neighbor's son parks his Repairs Of All Kinds, red and white van on the street where it will remain for the weekend. His father comes out of the house and greets his son--BB gun in hand; ready to shoot the woodpecker that is attacking his house.

The short lady in the blue house, whose name is "Tall" steps from her doorway onto her porch. She turns back and locks her door, walks to her Mercedes, gets in and drives away.

A man walking with a stick in hand--this he uses to scare dogs--circles the cul-de-sac on his afternoon walk.

The middle-aged man. two doors down, walks his large black dog by my house, stops and lets the dog water my flower beds.

The lady who organizes the "cul-de-sac" outdoor parties, and makes herself at home in my yard with her tables, chairs and grill, loads her girls into her van and backs out of her driveway. She waves at the old man who is now carrying a cage that holds a frightened squirrel. He waves. The children wave. The van drives away.

My sprinklers come on and water showers the beds of flowers. The azaleas gratefully drink, as do the yellow and salmon-colored lilies and the purple false-dragon-head.

The butterfly bushes, one purple, one white, sparkle with drops of water. The butterflies--monarch and yellow ones--drink from the wet leaves.

The robins and finches alternate bathing in the birdbath and sprinklers, wiggling their bodies and flapping their wings. The honey bees buzz from bloom to bloom, gathering nectar from begonias, Virginia bluebells and bleeding hearts. The slugs peak out from under rocks waiting for dark. They are eyeing the broad and tasty looking Hosta leaves.

The spent and shriveled blooms from the rose-of-Sharon bushes drop as new blooms open.

A chipmunk races across the yard and disappears from my view--headed for the porch.

As I lower the shade of my bedroom window, I see my husband, keys in hand, ever the peacemaker, walk to his car that is parked in front of our house. He gets in and moves it, all of three feet to our mailbox.

At the Retreat

The breeze from the open window moves the sheer white curtains in my upstairs bedroom bringing the smell of the ocean into the room. I hear the roar of the ocean from across the waterway, beyond the islands. A storm is coming.

The blue of the sky is disappearing as white billowy clouds blow in from the sea.

The tall pines, with branches only at the very top of their one hundred foot trunks, sway in the breeze that is growing in speed. The water oaks shake their tiny leaves loose. The leaves fall into the wind and are tossed about in swirls. The transplanted palmetto palms--unnatural this far north, slightly shiver in the increasing winds.

The mockingbird in the live oak dives deep into the gnarly branches in search of her nest where she will wait out the storm. The woodpecker folds his wings, and his red head disappears into his feathers while he clings to a branch deep within the mulberry.

In the distance I see the pond's surface--normally glass-like--ripple as the wind blows in. An egret and heron spread their wings and glide, just above the water, making their way to the island in the middle of the pond.

The oleanders' long stalks rattle like reeds tossing pink blossoms on the sidewalk.

The sky grows darker as black clouds roll in and lighting cracks the air, making me step back from the window. Sheets of rain sweep in. The car glistens in the downpour as its dirt washes away. The street fills with water that rushes to storm drains, while, in the yard, puddles form.

I close my upstairs window and go sit on the front porch in my light blue rocking chair and watch the thunder people play.

The Scene From My Upstairs Window

by Jane Ellen Holliday Wilson

It was a crystalline, magical moment
Standing there on my upstairs landing.
Pure *present*

No past
No future
Only gratitude

The married sensations
Of inner and outer
Of light and color
Nature and art blending together
As one

Outside
Snow and pines,
The leafless, grey maple branches
Upon which perched in perfect arrangement
Cardinals, woodpeckers and jays

Inside
Dangling from the windows
Three blown glass globes

Elegant fainting couch
Carved in the shape of a lion
Crouching paws, regal mane

A jungle of plants
Bright paintings of birds
All over the walls

So rare, so arresting I think
As I stand with laundry basket
Balanced on my hip

How often have I tried to manufacture
Such a scene?
And yet, here it is
Through the window

Out of nowhere

Nature has provided
A flawlessly executed
Artfully made
Vignette.

CHAPTER 13 A DOZEN EGGS AND A BOTTLE OF BUBBLY

GLENDA KOTCHISH and JANE WILSON

A Dozen Eggs and a Bottle of Bubbly

Jane Ellen Holliday Wilson

The move had been grueling. The two of them were exhausted and scared to death of what they had done—downsizing and moving into the heart of the city—by the time everything had been squeezed into the house, or hauled off to a rented storage unit they were both feeling as though they were a million years old.

And then the invitation came.

"What on earth am I supposed to do with this?"

It had been slipped through their mail slot at the front door (mail slots, yet another thing to grow accustom to) just two days before the event was to take place:

```
Easter Egg Hunt
Show up at 4:00
With a dozen eggs
And a bottle of bubbly
24 Holly Ave
No need to RSVP
```

Alice was stumped. What does it mean? She didn't even know who lived at 24 Holly Ave—four doors down the street—and the invitation listed no names at all—only the address.

Was she supposed to produce a child as well? That was not possible. Their barely-on-their-own bevy of children had produced no toddlers that could be commandeered to attend such an event. Was it an adults-only party? The

"Bubbly" implied that at least what adults did attend would be made merry. Should she wear a bonnet? A dress? Jeans? Was Harvey invited too, or was it just a girl thing? She couldn't ask the only neighbors she'd met so far. What if they hadn't been invited? Oh this was all very awkward!

And then there were the eggs—old-fashioned hand dyed hard-boiled the way her grandmother taught her, dyed with blueberries, onion skins and beets?

Or fancy plastic eggs filled with chocolates from that fashionable shop around the corner?

Or maybe they were to be organic, vegan, health conscious things.

Or something for grown-ups only? Or politically correct? Or politically incorrect? This was maddening. What to do?

Harvey said, "Alice, darling you are overthinking this. Just get some eggs and go."

"Aren't you coming Harvey? You can't let me go all by myself!" Alice sounded a bit more indignant than she meant to. This had been a long few weeks.

"Well," hedged Harvey.

"Or maybe you should be the one to get the eggs," she quipped.

"You really *have* lost your mind my sweet girl," Harvey laughed.

"Oh Harvey, you know I don't stand a prayer of you providing the eggs. Your solution to the whole dilemma would be just not to go. Then you wouldn't have to worry about it. But *it is* a party, after all, and somebody (mind you some mischievous somebody) has decided they want us there, and *by God and Easter* we're going—no matter how disastrous it is."

"That's my Alice. Never could resist an invitation. But please tell me I don't have to wear bunny ears."

"No bunny ears, Harvey. I promise I will not take it over the top. Now say you are coming."

"Could I ever deny you anything? Besides I'm too tired to argue."

That was it—with no more information than the invitation provided, Alice was determined to make a good showing with her new neighbors. She went to work.

A dozen eggs:

Three old fashioned hand dyed–blue, yellow, red

Three with silver dollars inside (appealing to both children and adults)

Three with tiny bubble blowers inside (appealing to children and some young-at-heart adults)

Three with fine French chocolate stuffed inside

All neatly fitted into an old egg carton decorated with Easter bunny clad paper on the outside and colored paper grass on the inside (very environmentally friendly, but festive still).

Next she went shopping for a good, but not too good bottle of sparkling wine. A lavender linen top, a straw hat and peg leg jeans completed the picture.

Harvey in tow—wearing his usual uniform of navy shorts and a short sleeve plaid shirt—looked miserable but at least provided a distraction.

At about 4:15 they walked down the block and rang the doorbell at #24, waiting anxiously for what they would find.

The door swung open onto a room full of Easter bunnies, chickens, adult-sized "girls" and "boys" in little girl Easter dresses and little boy sailor suits. Turned out, the party was hosted by the owner of the local costume store (mind you there were no costume stores in the suburbs from which Alice and Harvey had migrated).

Alice's promise that Harvey would not have to wear bunny ears flew out the window as each of them was handed a pair and welcomed joyfully into the raucous crowd of new neighbors (many of whom seemed to have been long into the *bubbly* by the time Harvey and Alice had arrived).

The old fashioned eggs, after being marveled over for their brilliant color, became egg salad, along with some from other guests. And the plastic eggs were added to a hoard of others hidden by a group of laughing men—Harvey, in his bunny ears, right in the middle of them all.

Later they were riotously hunted for hours on end, and then opened with even more hilarity after a barbecue supper was served.

And from that day on, Alice and Harvey called it their own personal Easter resurrection.

A Dozen Eggs and a Bottle of Bubbly

Glenda Mace Kotchish

Emma opened her mailbox on Good Friday to find an egg carton stuffed inside. A prank? She pulled the carton out of the mail box. It was one of those "cage free" organic containers made from recycled-paper no doubt. She cautiously opened it. Thankfully there were no eggs, fresh or rotten inside. There *was* a multi-colored half sheet of paper with scalloped edges. Hand scripted in ink was a message:

Fill me with eggs and bring a bottle of bubbly to the Stone House in Forest Park at 3:00 p.m. on Sunday. Don't worry--not an axe murderer.

E. B.
(Easter Bunny)

"Ha, how charming," Emma thought a little annoyed. She turned the carton over then gave it a good sniff. "No weed," she said out loud, then closed the carton, tucked it under her arm and took it in the house along with her other mail.

"This is a very mystifying invitation. Who is responsible? She thought, "Charles or Olivia?" her most quirky friends, or maybe it could be the new weird neighbors at the end of the block. It would be like them to do this--so goody, goody, and creative at every turn." She looked at her cat curled on the windowsill. "Well what think ye, Bella?" she said.

Bella, the old tabby cat raised her head at the sound of her name, blinked twice and yawn at Emma. "I take that as a yes?" Emma said. "OK, I'm in."

"So whomever it is--wants eggs. Humm…" Emma sat down in her favorite chair and stroked the cat. "What kind of eggs?" She thought for a while. "Nothing comes to mind. Maybe a little "bubbly" will help me come up with something."

She went to the pantry, rummaged around and discovered a bottle of sparkling wine with a label "perfect for sangria" --just add fruit. "Good idea," she thought. "Fruit it is--to make a proper afternoon drink." She set about chopping an orange and an apple, put them in a pitcher, added the wine and a touch of ginger ale. She stirred it gently and filled a wine goblet. She took a sip. "Delish. Now back to the matter of eggs."

Emma returned to her chair. The sun was shining in the window and Bella was snoring. After a while the glass was empty and Emma still had no egg ideas--nothing.

"OK, time to get serious. I'll check the Internet. There's gotta be something interesting out there. She went to her desk, opened her laptop and started surfing. She found an abundance of eggs--colored eggs, paper eggs, plastic eggs, eggs in shells, eggs out of shells, eggs--just the shells--pages and pages of eggs.

"Jesus, Mary and Joseph." Emma mumbled. "Let's take this to another level--something as mystifying as the invitation--get into the game, girl."

She went to her bookcase and searched until she found the book she was looking for--an old journal from her time spent at the commune. She turned the pages. "Ah, here it is, our experiments."

She picked up the phone and called Charles.

"Hello friend!" she cheerfully spoke into the phone. "I'm in the need for some *special ingredients.*"

'Well, well Emma--what fiendish scheme are you up too?" Charles inquired.

"Just a little special Easter surprise, for a party. Can you let me have a few of your plants from the greenhouse? I just need a tiny bit--some samplings really--that's all." Emma asked.

" Sure, for an old friend--anything. What exactly do you need?'

Emma consulted her book and gave Charles the list. "That will do it. Should I come by tomorrow and pick them up?"

"Sure, tomorrow around noon is fine; come to the greenhouse," Charles replied. "Oh and Emma."

"Yes, Charles?"

"Just be careful, OK?"

"Pshaw, Charles. Don't be a party pooper. It's just a little fun, that's all," responded Emma.

When they hung up Emma set about planning her eggs. "Let's see, I'll need my egg cooker--where is that?" She searched through her cabinets until she found the little gadget her brother gave her. He loved kitchen gadgets, and thought everyone else shared his enthusiasm for the latest gizmo. "It is a nifty little cooker," Emma admitted to herself. She placed six eggs in the rack. "I'll have to make two batches," she told Bella whose curiosity had brought her into the kitchen.

Bella crouched as though about to leap. "Don't even think about jumping up on this counter. This is off limits--as you well know," Emma warned.

Bella sat back on her haunches and curled her tail around herself. "Good girl," Emma remarked. "Now, just take this plastic cylinder which has this little spiky thing in the bottom and punch a hole in the top of each egg. Why? you ask, Bella."

Bella looked up. "Well, this little hole allows the steam to escape from the egg as it cooks and there is the bonus of a tiny hole in which I can inject some flavoring and color for the inside of the eggs. That's unusual, right? White eggs on the outside but color and special herbs and flavors on the inside." Emma continued telling Bella.

Emma found the food coloring and laid out everything she'd need for dying the eggs. "Off to the greenhouse, tomorrow I can cook up some amazing, magical mystery eggs."

Saturday 12:00 p.m.

Charles, dressed in turquoise, geometric, mandala harem pants and a tie-dyed t-shirt, opened the greenhouse door and greeted Emma with a smile.

"What's with the outfit? You had to dig pretty deep in the cedar chest to find those," Emma said as she stood on tiptoes and gave Charles a big hug.

"Well, as a matter of fact, I did--and all in honor of you my dear. Since we are "experimenting" today--we are experimenting, aren't we? I thought I should dress for the part. Come in. Everything is ready.

Emma entered the greenhouse and stood for a while looking at the rows of plants, flowers, vegetables, herbs-- uncommon all. If there was something unusual you wanted, then Chaz Arboretum was the place to go.

"So where do you keep your *specialty* plants these days?" Emma hooked her arm in Charles'.

He smiled down at her. "Right this way, a cozy spot in the back. But first, let me lock the door." He strode to the front door and turned the lock. "There. We're closed today but you never know when someone might think otherwise and disturb us. No interruptions today. Just like old times, a little trip down memory lane," he laughed.

"Oh stop. You and your puns. I hadn't intended on sampling the merchandise," Emma laughed.

"What? No, I won't have it. If you want samples, then you must sample--that's the rule," Charles insisted. He stood in place, arms crossed.

Emma sighed. "Oh alright. It's been a long time since I've partaken, so just a little for me."

Charles put his arm around Emma. "Let's be off. You'll love the room I have set up--cushions, lava lamps, a canopy--everything for our comfort and magical mystery tour."

Together they walked through the labyrinth of plants, rooms and through doorways. Emma handed Charles her journal. He led her into the *specialty* room and closed the door behind them.

Sunday 3:00 p.m.

Emma arrived at The Stone House at promptly 3:00 pm on Sunday in her gray linen dress, straw hat, sandals and white gloves. In one hand, she held the egg carton and in the other a bottle of French champagne. No one was in sight.

"Odd," Emma thought as she climbed the stairs to the front door. It was open, so she walked in. The Stone House had one large room with a bank of doors on the back wall. Behind the doors were small rooms used for storage, a restroom and a kitchen. Emma knew this place well because she had been here many times. The community used the house for meetings and neighborhood projects like the Christmas Mother gift distribution, summer solstice sky observations and a way station for winter sleighing in the park.

The room was empty except for a single table in the middle. She crossed the floor to the table. On it was a red egg. She looked around confused. So, she picked up the egg and turned it over. On the back was traced in script: "crack me."

Emma rolled her eyes and pursed her lips, annoyed, but a little apprehensive, too--about blindly following instructions and accepting invitations from persons unknown.

"Well, I've come this far, I may as well crack the damn thing," she thought. She tapped the egg on the table and it nearly dissolved in her hand--the shell, if shell it was, dissipated into red powder and wafted through the room. A tiny piece of paper was all that remained, and written in the familiar scripted handwriting were these words:

Emma, so glad you came. Bring the basket from under the table, your eggs and bottle of bubbly (you did bring eggs and bubbly, I hope) and open the third door to your left. See you soon. E.B.

"This is absurd," Emma said out loud. Her apprehension was increasing. "Yet *another* instruction," she thought. She raised the skirt of the tablecloth and there was indeed a basket under the table. She pulled it out and placed it on the table. Inside were a champagne flute, a tiny flashlight and a key.

"OK," she said as she placed her egg carton and champagne in the basket. She stood and walked over to the third door.

Her hand shook a little as she put the key into the keyhole. "Should I really do this?" she wondered. "Well I can at least open the door and then decide," she thought as she turned the key. She pulled the door open. She saw a staircase of stone steps. The walls--also stone--were changing colors from blue, violet, red, orange, yellow, to green. And there was music--violins-- Mozart softly playing. A sweet scent drifted through the door. Her apprehension left as she started down the stairs, the music drawing her and the colors playing gently on the walls. "I'll be at the party soon," she thought.

The stairs turned and spiraled down, growing wider at each turn. When she finally reached the bottom, she was in a room with a high ceiling from which a chandelier hung. Candles were burning and the smell of wax filled the room. She noticed that the light show had changed from the full color spectrum to only violets and reds. There was no one in sight. Emma glanced around the room. Immediately beneath the glowing chandelier-- someone had placed a yellow settee, two side tables and a rug of purples.

"Wow, so mysterious," Emma whispered. She walked to the settee. On one table was an origami egg. On the other was a linen napkin, folded on a silver tray. She settled herself on the settee. The music stopped, as did the lights on the walls.

"What now?" she thought. "God, I hope this is not a serial killer or something awful," and a little bit of fear twisted in her stomach. She sat for a while and finally picked up the origami egg and held it in her gloved hand. As she turned it--the egg began unfolding. In each fold there was a word.

"What's this?" she asked, out loud.

The script was tiny and the room dark. She reached in her basket to get the flashlight.

"Let's see what exactly is written here," she said and began to study each word.

It read:

Emma, please open your champagne, drink some bubbly while you enjoy the music. There are chocolates under the napkin. Help yourself. Then come through the door behind you.

Bring your glass and your basket. Your color is red so follow the red light. E.B.

When she finished reading the note, it dissipated in her hand. Music--Mozart, once again, began to play--this time a piano in a minor key. Emma couldn't name the tune but it was familiar. She stood up and expertly opened the bottle of champagne. She poured herself a glass and settled on the settee. She sipped at her champagne thankful that she had brought the kind she liked. She listened to the music and watched the colors ripple around the room. "A deranged person wouldn't play this music," she consoled herself, trying not to feel closed in.

The music stopped. Emma waited, then put her glass

in her basket. "Time to proceed?" she asked the empty room. She picked up her basket and walked to the door behind her. It was unlocked. She opened the door and heard music--once again, Mozart--peaceful and soft. Ahead of her was a long hallway with arched ceilings--like a tunnel. Every ten feet or so there was an alcove in the wall about waist high--like something in a church fashioned for a saintly statue. Each alcove was lit with a soft light of blue, violet or red.

"Oh my. Lovely," Emma whispered. She walked down the stone hallway. "Wait, this reminds me of something." She said out loud. "A basket, a yellow (well red) brick road…" she laughed feeling a little woozy. Touching the walls with her gloved hand, she slowly made her way to the first alcove glowing red.

In the alcove was a woven basket made of straw. In the straw were eggs and a little note.

"Take one and leave one." E.B.

Emma selected an egg from her carton and placed it in the straw. The red light made her white egg glow. "Lovely," Emma said. Then she selected an egg from the straw. On it someone had painted a dragon.

"Ah, now this is a proper Easter egg hunt," Emma smiled and continued down the tunnel and stopped at each red alcove to take and leave an egg until all the eggs she'd brought were gone and replaced with others.

At the final alcove, she looked around and saw several doors. One glowed red. "I guess that's my door," she thought and made her way to it.

She walked up several steps, turned the brass handle and pushed--just as the lights went out behind her. The door was heavy and didn't give easily. After some effort and with rising anxiety and not a little anger, she finally pushed the door open and stepped, to her wonderment into the sunlight. Emma let out a sigh of relief. But as she looked around--there was no one there--no one to greet her--no party. The sun was getting low and shadows long. How long had she been in the tunnel? Where was she now?

"Hello. Anyone here?" she called. Only birds tweeted. She was at the edge of the wooded area of the park. She made her way to the pathway and started walking. Finally arriving back at the Stone House--again, no one was around and now the house was locked.

"So weird--did I miss something somewhere in the tunnel?" Feeling a little put out and a little foolish she said, "I could have stayed at home with my cat and had better company." She glanced down at the basket in her hand and saw the eggs she'd gathered and recalled the white eggs she'd left in the tunnel. Her eyes narrowed and a small, insidious smile curled at her lips.

At home, she set the basket on the table--twelve eggs, half a bottle of champagne, a flashlight. In the tunnel she had chosen the eggs almost randomly as the light was undulating in shades of red, and images were deceptive to the eye. She examined the eggs closely now, one after another and lined them up in a row.

The dragon egg was her favorite--red and gold flames, purple eyes and silver scales. The detail was amazing. In sharp contrast was the clown--black and white with a scowl.

"Clowns are so creepy," Emma said and put the egg down.

Next was the orange lily--quite an angry looking flower, if flowers can be angry; followed by the beautiful but deadly belladonna plant. The leaves were green, the flowers--purple and bell shape. The berries were a shiny dark purple.

"Such a coincidence to have selected an egg with the belladonna plant," she thought. "Take one, give one", she said and smiled. "I certainly won't be taking a bite of you, little belladonna egg," she said.

Then there was the Egyptian eye egg--a line drawing on a yellow background. Was this the infamous evil eye?

An assortment of insect eggs followed: the bo weevil--a blackish beetle, the assassin bug--a burnt sienna color with its piercing beak positioned between its front legs. "Such a nasty little thing you are," Emma said. "You literally suck the life out of your prey," and she sat it aside.

There was the ill-tempered yellow jacket on a purple background. A tiger was exceptionally rendered--teeth bared. There was only one bird--a vulture, ugly creature. There were two red eggs without images but the red was deep as blood drops. One was in swirls like pinwheels. And lastly there was a daisy on a blue background. Unlike the other foreboding, nefarious eggs, this one was the picture of happiness.

Emma weighed the eggs in her hand, hard-boiled all. "A shame," she thought. These will spoil and the images with them. Perhaps the images were only decals applied to the eggs, which would account for the detail. These would have made a lovely arrangement in a glass bowl. She moved them to the mantel above the fireplace to display for a day or two.

"What an odd way to spend a Sunday afternoon. I wonder who the other guests were, if there were any. Perhaps I was the only guest. Even more curious, who was the host? Who is E. B.?" These thoughts continued to puzzle her as she went to bed.

Pulling the covers over herself, Emma wondered, "What is to become of the eggs that I have so carefully prepared--so plain on the outside but so colorful and magical on the inside? Has another guest chosen my eggs? Are they now looking at them on a table? Perhaps he or she, at this very moment, is daring to crack one, and discovering the color and fragrance within. And if so, will he or she dare to take a bite and taste the flavoring? Would anyone meet and experience the Virgin Mary, or feel the glow of Angels Trumpet, or the sweet, mind-bending Belladonna. Perhaps the illusive E.B. has the eggs, and is even now taking a little journey in another sort of tunnel, courtesy of me, Emma."

"Tasty little eggies, E.B., just for you." Emma turned off the light and closed her eyes--smiling.

She whispered softly, "E. B., you will reveal yourself to me by morning as I have my coffee and check the news. Maybe--maybe not." And she fell into a deep, deep sleep.

GLENDA KOTCHISH and JANE WILSON

CHAPTER 14 AND THEN THERE'S LOVE

GLENDA KOTCHISH and JANE WILSON

Every Morning That They Could

Jane Ellen Holliday Wilson

Every morning that he could, he ran along the sculpture garden nature trail, usually around 7:00. That would give him time to get back to the campus before 9:00 classes—freshmen classes usually, much as he loved teaching them, they *were* the mindless classes. Poor freshmen were the ones who had to get up for the early lectures. He could teach those classes in his sleep at this point in his career, but, unlike most of his colleagues, he still kept them on his roster (instead of passing them off to graduate assistants) because he felt it helped him to stay *fresh*, and remember what it was like to be so young and impressionable.

Each morning, he would arrive at the gate; punch in the code given him by his buddy Carl, the garden's executive director. He'd said to come around 7:00; no one would be there then. So he came, usually a little after 7:00. He just couldn't resist that snooze button.

He would ease into his run by first sauntering over to the statue of Zeus. Once he had said good morning to this testosterone infused and massively confident bronze behemoth of a guy, he would begin to pick up speed and head off toward the nature trail.

The run was his salvation. It gave him time to reflect on his life, his next scholarly work, and the gradual progression toward letting go of the pain of Anna's abrupt departure.

"You're just not man enough for me any more. Why, you won't even engage in a good fight these days. There's no fire in you. I need a real man." She had said this as she walked out the door--this time for the last time. She was off to meet some newer, younger *treasure* she had found.

Somehow, he hadn't seen it coming at all, she always came back, but this time she was gone for good. And so it must be true after all, he really wasn't man enough for the girl–the gods only knew. "Zeus, please tell me what sort of man I need to be to please a woman *these days*," he often asked as he broke into his first full stride.

The run helped to assuage the unfulfilled desire that had been left in Anna's wake as well. Well, at least until he happened upon *her*—that fine-boned little sprite of a creature—always elusive. Beautiful in her sadness, or that was how she seemed to him—very beautiful, and yet sad somehow.

Carl must have given her the code too, or maybe she worked in one of the shops on the grounds. It seemed that she had a favorite statue too--Pomona, goddess of fruitful abundance. He had looked it up after he caught sight of her that morning a while back. He saw her standing there before Pomona with her hands cupping her face. As he drew nearer he could hear her weeping. So she was a troubled soul too, but oh so intriguing. He forced himself to push on quickly that day, hoping that she never noticed that someone had caught her in her grief.

But, it was the *yoga* that really enthralled him. She had a spot by the labyrinth, in the corner, under a live oak tree. This is where she would go to do yoga after stopping in on Pomona. What were they–mudras and asanas and salutations–sun salutations, and cobras, and downward facing dogs, and warriors one and two, and all that mumbo jumbo? He had to confess, he had researched this stuff too--just in case he ever got the nerve to speak.

If he timed it right, he could catch a good bit of the routine as he approached the spot. This morning he wondered if he *would* ever get the nerve. Just say, "Hi." Just "Hi," for God's sake. You fool.

Every morning that she could, she practiced her yoga in her favorite spot by the labyrinth that sat just off the sculpture garden nature trail, usually around 7:00. That would give her time to rush back to school for her first art class of the day—the freshmen were always first (or should she call them fresh-women, better yet fresh-girls--silly things). They would troop in wearing their already slouchy uniforms, grade by grade, all through the day. Occasionally one might have some talent in spite of her already privileged position in life.

Carl had given her the pass code while she was teaching a college level art class for the garden. They had gotten to know each other well during her tenure there, and he had encouraged her to come—around 7:00 he had said. It's the best time. So she came, usually a little before 7:00. She was an early riser.

She would start with a meditative walk through the garden, meandering up to visit Pomona's marble statue for just a moment. Drinking in her gentle form, her perfectly ordered hair, her air of confidence, she only wished she could be more like this nymph.

She needed that confidence to face the girls each day. And their hovering parents--poor things, they actually thought they were in some kind of control of those wild creatures.

Her yoga, and Pomona helped her to open to her own creativity. Her weavings were gaining local and even regional renown. Perhaps in a year or two she would be able to quit this maddening job and devote all of her time to her art.

She would already be doing this if Paul had stayed. That was their plan. He would take his place in the family law practice, and she would stay home, host dinner parties and work on her weavings. The plan, that is, until things started falling apart. It seemed she could do nothing right. She would choose the wrong china, or place the wrong dinner guests next to each other. (Who knew their mothers hadn't spoken in over 20 years?) "And what were those weird things she had made and hung all over the walls?"

Finally one day, Paul came home and announced he was leaving, and taking the family china with him. "You're just too mousy, and clumsy, and a lousy hostess. If I don't get Grandmother Hannah's china out of here fast, you'll break every dish, you ill-bred idiot." And with that he was gone. Funny, she hadn't broken a dish since the day he walked out.

Still she felt so thrown away—so incapable--a failure; so unlovable. The yoga helped her to process all of this pain as well. And it helped manage her longings too. Until that tall handsome guy ran by, that is. Who on earth was *he*—a terrible distraction, that was for sure—his ruddy complexion, that godlike bone structure and curly, auburn hair tied back in a ponytail? She wondered what he did at the garden; probably a gardener or something.

When she saw him, her spine would begin to tingle (an unfortunate happening in the middle of cobra pose). No matter how hard she tried to stay focused, he would always throw her off. She thought him very much like that bronze of Zeus she had seen him standing in front of one day when she was late. Zeus-like he was when he invaded her thoughts in the middle of art class, or even once, in her dreams.

Her cheeks colored as she considered again whether he had seen her that morning she broke down in front of Pomona, the morning after the divorce papers were served. If he had, then blessedly, he moved on without a word. She wondered now if ever there would be a word between them.

Perhaps she could start with a smile. Would it be too much to just start with a smile?

Today?

Yes, today she would try *a smile*.

"Hello," he said.

Heart thumping.

"Hi," she returned.

Every morning that they could manage, they made their way to the sculpture garden nature trail, usually around 7:00. In one hand, his walking cane, in the other, always, her hand. They would make their way first by Zeus, then Pomona, then on to the bench by the labyrinth. Carl and the children had it put there when his knee replacements and the continuing ravages of arthritis made it hard for him to move about.

Then they would sit on the bench, snuggle a bit, and talk.

GLENDA KOTCHISH and JANE WILSON

The Piano

Glenda Mace Kotchish

There it was, the full page ad--"Going Out of Business"--City Piano. Angie showed it to her lover, Warren.

"I've always wanted to learn to play the piano. One year for Christmas I asked for piano lessons. And piano lessons I got. But we didn't have a piano."

"How did you practice?" He asked.

"I practiced on a small electric organ that we had at home, and I went to the church one day a week to use the piano there, when I could get a ride."

"How did it go?" He asked.

"My Dad got sick and had a hard time working so I gave it up. Mama thought my playing was so tiresome that she moved the organ to the screened in porch. It was hard to practice in the winter, out there in the cold. I wore the big black coat that she kept hanging on the hook by the back door," she said.

"Whose coat?" Warren asked.

"My mother's."

He said, "You should buy the piano--for yourself. I'll go with you."

Something entirely for herself--a novel idea. In her marriage, before this new lover, it was tit for tat. If she got something, no matter how small--her former husband got something of equal or greater value.

She looked around her new apartment--sparsely furnished. She had let her former husband have all the furniture, dishes, pots and pans, appliances, everything including the house when she finally left. Everything in this small one bedroom apartment was newly acquired--

mostly second hand--the kitchen table and two chairs, the end tables and coffee table--the lamp without a lampshade. The sofa was new--an extravagance. It was lovely--very deep so that two people could lie side by side with a queen size pull out bed for company. Her mattress and box springs and bed frame were new. Only she and he had slept there. She'd made the bedspread and curtains to match from sheets. She'd filled the sheets for her bedspread with batting providing a soft, cool effect. The print was irises, purple and greens on a white background--Iris, her middle name--all hers. The spread always made her smile because of that.

Now, she imagined the piano taking up a space in the living room.

"Ok. They're open now. Let's go look," She said.

So they did. There were grands and baby-grands, consoles and uprights. She walked among them. He followed. He played a few notes on each one she stopped at. And then there it was--the Kawaii--black lacquer with no front legs. The keyboard floated from the base in midair--a console with good sound. It was perfect. It was so her!

And so it was she bought her longed for piano. It was delivered while she was at work. The apartment manager let the company in. When she came home from work that day, it was in her living room--keyboard open with a red-felt cloth laid over the keys.

He stepped in behind her, smiled and said "May I play you a love song?"

ABOUT THE AUTHORS

GLENDA MACE KOTCHISH

Glenda Kotchish owns an art center in Richmond, Virginia where every month there's a party with new artwork, food and wine. How fun is that!

She has a banking and IT background and found herself illustrating some quite boring documents to make them, well less boring. She writes about everything because, everything can be a story. She loves short stories and believes that someday they may weave themselves into a novel. Favorite short story author: Neil Gaiman. "He's amazing."

JANE ELLEN HOLLIDAY WILSON

Jane Wilson is a philanthropic *thought partner*, which means, she helps philanthropists consider how best to use their various resources of time, talent, influence and money. Janie has a mantra that she likes to use: kindness+courage+gratitude=abundance.
Isn't that what we all crave—an abundant life?

Her *abundant* life has been full of so many things; an early career in interior space planning and design; two beautiful daughters off doing interesting things with their lives; a second career in the social sector; and a second family that includes four more delightful young adults (and of course their fabulous father).

In the midst of all of this, she began to write fiction, poetry, memoir and so forth. "It just came over me like a gentle spring storm." She has a novel and two novellas in the works, along with an anthology about wandering with her parents through their many years of dementia.